W9-CTY-855

THE PENGUIN POETS

AUTOBIOGRAPHIES

Alfred Corn has published five previous books of poetry and a collection of essays, all with Viking Penguin. He has won a number of prizes and fellowships for his work, including the Guggenheim, the NEA, and an Award in Literature from the Academy and Institute of Arts and Letters. In 1988 he was named a Fellow of the Academy of American Poets. He has taught poetry-writing at Yale, the University of Cincinnati, U.C.L.A., and Columbia, and he is a frequent contributor to *The New York Times Sunday Book Review*, *Washington Post Book World*, and *The Nation*. He lives in New York City.

AUTOBIOGRAPHIES

POEMS BY
ALFRED CORN

PENGUIN BOOKS

PENGUIN BOOKS
Published by the Penguin Group
Viking Penguin, a division of Penguin Books USA Inc.,
375 Hudson Street, New York, New York 10014, U.S.A.
Penguin Books Ltd, 27 Wrights Lane,
London W8 5TZ, England
Penguin Books Australia Ltd, Ringwood,
Victoria, Australia
Penguin Books Canada Ltd, 10 Alcorn Avenue, Suite 300,
Toronto, Ontario, Canada M4V 3B2
Penguin Books (N.Z.) Ltd, 182–190 Wairau Road,
Auckland 10, New Zealand

Penguin Books Ltd, Registered Offices:
Harmondsworth, Middlesex, England

First published in the United States of America
by Viking Penguin, a division of
Penguin Books USA Inc. 1992
Published in Penguin Books 1993

10 9 8 7 6 5 4 3 2 1

Page ix constitutes an extension of this copyright page.

LIBRARY OF CONGRESS CATALOGING IN PUBLICATION DATA
Corn, Alfred, 1943–
    Autobiographies: poems/Alfred Corn.
      p.   cm.
    ISBN 0 14 05.8690 3
    I. Title.
  PS3553.0655A95   1993
  811'.54—dc20   92-1002

Printed in the United States of America
Set in Sabon
Designed by Ann Gold

FOR WALTER BROWN

Continuing gratitude

'O frati,' dissi, 'che per cento milia
   Perigli siete giunti a l'occidente,
   A questa tanto picciola vigilia
De' nostri sensi ch'è del rimanente
   Non vogliate negar l'esperïenza,
   Diretro al sol, del mondo sanza gente.
Considerate la vostra semenza:
   Fatti non foste a viver come bruti,
   Ma per seguir virtute e canoscenza.'
      —Dante, *Inferno*, Canto XXVI

               The sea
Severs not only lands but also selves.
   —Stevens,
      "The Comedian as the Letter C"

ACKNOWLEDGMENTS

The author wishes to acknowledge the first publication of the following poems, with thanks to the editors of these magazines:

Antaeus: Section 14 of "1992."

The Cincinnati Poetry Review: "Equal and Opposite" (under the title "The Law of Reciprocal Force").

Grand Street: "Contemporary Culture and the Letter 'K.' "

The Kenyon Review: Sections 12, 15, and 18 of "1992."

The Nation: "After Rilke" and "Resolutions."

The New Republic: "Cannot Be a Tourist" and "My Neighbor, the Distinguished Count."

The New Yorker: "A Village Walk under Snow" and "Coventry."

The Paris Review: "La Madeleine" and Sections 1, 10, and 17 of "1992."

Partisan Review: Section 8 of "1992."

Ploughshares: "Somerset Alcaics."

Poetry: "Infernal Regions and the Invisible Girl."

Salmagundi: "The Jaunt."

Southwest Review: "Right and Left Hand."

– –

"Right and Left Hand" was published in limited edition by Friday Imprints at the Logan Elm Press, The Ohio State University.

"Somerset Alcaics" was published in limited edition by Sea Cliff Press.

"Infernal Regions and the Invisible Girl" was collected in *The Best Poems of 1991*, Mark Strand and David Lehman, editors.

– –

Grateful acknowledgment is due to the NEA for fellowship support during the period when some of these poems were written, as well as for maintaining its commitment to freedom of expression.

Residences at the Mishkenot Sha'ananim in Jerusalem; the Djerassi Foundation; the Poet's House in New Harmony, Indiana; at Yaddo; and at the Thurber House in Columbus were very helpful in the completion of this book, and I would like to express thanks again here.

CONTENTS

AUTOBIOGRAPHIES

A VILLAGE WALK UNDER SNOW

Roiling flakes,
The lunge of a million carousels
In free fall makes
Frame houses' old pastels

By contrast bright
As fresh enamel; while that Ford
(In negative white)
Reveals the silkenly scored

Streamlines wind
Tunnels were designed to test.
Cold weather, friend,
Truest if not the best,

Is seeing saving—
This tufted pine branch, thick with spume
As a poised shaving
Brush or egret's plume,

Mine to keep?
And those post-Xmas Xmas trees
Fallen asleep
In snow and left to freeze

On kelp-strewn sands of
The vacant public beach. . . . Enough
That wheeling bands of
Gulls patrol a rough-

Hewn, bile-dark sea,
Rising to meet the falling sky
Where gulls are free,
Hovering, to dive or cry.

(A bold one dives
Right now, just past my head—one more
Of those close shaves
Outdoors is noted for.)

Jumbo lace,
A complex tire-track hems the path
My steps retrace
In the homeward aftermath—

Gray skies, bare trees,
Houses seen through veils of snow,
Affording ease
Good for an hour or so.

CANNOT BE A TOURIST

Not casually. Within two days
Streets and vista are mine forever,
Some last few wisps of jet lag clearing
As senses expand to occupy
A space already second nature.

How many facts, though, work against
Staying put. A rented house;
An unknown language stumbled over;
Formal obligations, debts,
In taut suspense back where we vote.

Brought home so often, still the dried
Pages of the journal are more
Compelling than they have a right,
Much reasonable right, to be.
Only alight on them and now

Ancestor olives near Delphi
Stand in an oddly youthful trance;
The vines outside Siena, leaf
By jagged, gold-veined, classic leaf,
Outline the sun in a dust of earth;

Bronze, coal-green, the Haitian bantam
Stalks a wall spilled over with red
Bougainvillea; or Quai Voltaire's
Streaked pediment enshrines a crush
Of half-nude marble, artist-cohorts

Living it up in their garret (the Seine
By night, each lamp secreted in oyster
Mist). . . . Facts be damned: some part follows
Hereafter and continues. At home
Where the heart enlarged by affection is,

Whoever could not be a tourist
Shuts the door pro forma only—
Aware, even so, that form's good practice
For firm conclusions, holding steady
When time says, "Bid the earth farewell."

MY NEIGHBOR, THE
DISTINGUISHED COUNT

At first thinking it was harmless
Enough, I told myself I had pints
To spare, so why refuse a simple favor?
Hannah could have turned him away at the door,
But I didn't think that was necessary.
I'd always liked his mother and father
(Whom he grew sadly to resemble less
As months passed, his condition progressing).
The visits came bearably seldom,
And no one could have brought everything
Off more smoothly. Afterwards I'd feel calmer,
Drowsy, reconciled. Easy to see why
People once regularly bled themselves
For medical reasons, though of course
That was a cure normally reserved for men,
Who labor under greater pressures than we.
Easy, too, for one to think of donor service
As the good deed for the day—thy neighbor
As thyself, no?—a neighbor so visibly
In need, his pale brow furrowed, an electric
Tic active at the corner of the mouth.
Thoughts less reassuring surfaced later
When what he meant as compensation arrived,
The flowers, touring car idling outside,
Heart-shaped boxes of intricate chocolates,
Young Burgundies, spring lamb nicely done up.

Why did the visits multiply? No doubt
There had been other clients beforehand,
But perhaps they moved or died, who can say?
Or else he'd concluded I was, for the moment,
A likely vintage and a pleasant temperature.
One afternoon I brought myself to ask.

"I come to you, dearest, because you think
Of me. An irresistible summons."
Manners: how tell an acquaintance serene
In the conviction of having been your constant
Preoccupation for how long now that,
In fact, you hardly ever thought of him?
Chided jokingly, could he read minds?
He answered, even better than that, he could read
Signs. It seemed I'd left them everywhere.
And true messages always reached their addressee,
Wasn't it so? From this I knew the mere facts
Of our erratic situation counted for nothing
When placed beside his own inner persuasions.

He told me he'd been seeing more "signs" than ever,
And certainly he came to me more and more often,
Insisting I call him Tony, as his friends did.
I tactfully refused. When dealing with
Obsession, as a rule the safest plan
Is to maintain a strict formality.
Yet it occurred to me at some point symptoms
Might creep up with no warning. You would be
Quite unaware of new expressive habits
Connected, *he* said, to your daydreams—which,
In this case, were also traps. I must outwit them.
Have you ever tried *not* to think of a face
Or a voice, going over each confused tangle
On the mental loom to make sure the banned
Thread of reference doesn't appear in it?
How often I longed to stay profoundly asleep
And never be conscious again. . . . Waking,
I brooded on little but how to stop our meetings,
A rebellion no doubt proving just how much his
I was. For what demonstrates more clearly

The power of a creator than fierce resistance
From his creature? If alive, it will be free.
Free, it will insist on its own ideas—
And so, at last, have to be disciplined.

Lately, there's been another turn of the screw.
His chauffeur arrives with a silver cover
Under which lies a rat, spitted and roasted.
Or his gardener will leave a fistful of poison ivy
Tied with catgut in the mailbox. And then, the dresses,
Too small, too large, jaundice yellow, black violet.
Now, it's hopeless, no hour passes without thoughts
I've given up trying to sidestep or quench—
Which he has taken as license to appear
At all hours, day or night, and send, with thanks,
More frequent tokens of declining esteem.
I gather from what he says (we sit, we chat)
I'm not what I used to be, his visits, indeed,
A gesture of sentimental gallantry.
Apparently there's someone else less . . . shopworn.
Yesterday I asked, in a voice admittedly weak
(The constant drain), *why* he still bothered to call.
"Because, my dear, you haven't stopped thinking of me."
I blushed (faintly), he smiled, and when he left there was—
Where? Oh yes, the kitchen—a coiled blood sausage,
Old, wizened, utterly dried out, resting
On a small hand mirror. I remember this now
Only because I can't help doing so, aware
Of the acrid little joke: that, according
To his iron code of gamesmanship, I have
Just authorized another courtesy call.
In full knowledge also (hideous necklace of sores
That no longer heal, veins like blackened vines!)
That today he will come for the last time.

My quaint request is that the coup de grâce
Be administered by himself alone and not
By any of his troop of haggard followers
Who have begun to congregate outside.
Thick as autumn leaves ready for the bonfire,
They throng my doorstep, basset eyes pleading;
And, without giving their names, pronounce my own,
A silken cajolery drolly intoned, as if—
As if they were old friends I'm about to rejoin.
And then, this driving pain in my eyeteeth,
This thirst. . . . Well, you see, I want my turn, too.
A country mile off, I saw and felt the change.
It has the magnetism of all dimly grasped ideals.
Surely by now no one can say I am not deserving?
I understand the problems and am willing to work.

Look, he has arrived. Hannah's white cap vanishes
Down the dark passage and is replaced by his face
Floating in the gloom like a full moon, eyes lowered,
His left hand dangling a gold watch on its long chain.
Never have I seen so much, nor ever felt so deeply—
Hence the sudden piercing intimation of what I am
One day to be, this twilit picture of discretion, the set
Of his features calm as an engraving of one who lets words
Of gratitude pass in silence as he settles to the task.

EQUAL AND OPPOSITE

As soon take on a wildcat as tangle
    with the pine, crouching in keen alertness
six cold decades on a windy outcrop.
    Tested by storm and stone, it knows its strengths:
scaled bark, needle, cone, the evergreen rose
    and shaped its taproot to the fissure found.
Those opponents taught the pine who it was?
    The pine says such debts are reciprocal.

"Before I stood in growing defiance,
    wind was airy nothing, insubstantial
to itself. And these roots that prise apart
    the grip of living rock worked to inspire
a fine resistance in the passive stone.
    I fought to make them something fierce to fight.
In deadlock embrace, with zeal and gusto,
    I have shown my opponents who they were."

CONTEMPORARY CULTURE AND THE LETTER "K"

First inroads were made in our 19-aughts
(Foreshadowed during the last century by nothing
More central than "Kubla Khan," Kipling, Greek
Letter societies, including the grotesque KKK—
Plus the kiwi, koala, and kookaburra from Down Under)
When certain women applied to their moist eyelids
A substance pronounced *coal* but spelled *kohl,*
Much of the effect captured on Kodak film
With results on and off camera now notorious.
They were followed and sometimes chased by a platoon
Of helmeted cutups styled the *Keystone Kops,* who'd
Freeze in the balletic pose of the letter itself,
Left arm on hip, leg pointed back at an angle,
Waiting under klieg lights next a worried kiosk
To put the kibosh on Knickerbocker misbehavior.
Long gone, they couldn't help when that hirsute royal
King Kong arrived to make a desperate last stand,
Clinging from the Empire State, swatting at biplanes,
Fay Wray fainting away in his leathern palm
As in the grip of African might. Next, marketing
Stepped up with menthol tobacco and the brand name
Kool, smoked presumably by models and archetypes
Superior in every way to Jukes and Kallikaks.
By then the race was on, if only because
Of German *Kultur*'s increasing newsworthiness
On the international front. The nation that had canned
Its Kaiser went on to sponsor debuts for the hero
Of *Mein Kampf,* Wotan of his day, launching thunderbolts
And Stukas, along with a new social order astonishing
In its industrial efficiency. His annexing
Of Bohemia cannot have been spurred by reflecting
That after all Prague had sheltered the creator
And in some sense alter-ego of Josef K.,
Whose trial remained a local fact until the fall

Of the Empire of a Thousand Years, unheard of in "Amerika"
Of the Jazz Age. But musicians Bix Beiderbecke and Duke
Ellington somehow always took care to include the token
Grapheme in their names, for which precaution fans
Of certain priceless '78s can only be grateful.
They skipped and rippled through a long post-war glow
Still luminous in the memory of whoever recalls
Krazy Kat, Kleenex, Deborah Kerr, Korea, Kool-Aid,
And Jack Kennedy. Small wonder if New York had
A special feeling for the theme, considering radical
Innovations of De Kooning, Kline, and Rothko. This last
Can remind us that bearers of the letter often suffered
Bereavement and despair (*cf.* Chester Kallman) and even,
As with Weldon Kees, self-slaying. Impossible not to see
Symptoms of a malaise more widespread still in a culture
That collects kitsch and Krugerrands, with a just-kids lifestyle
Whose central shrine is the shopping mall—K-Mart, hail to thee!
To "Kuntry Kitchen," "Kanine Kennels," and a host of other
Kreative misspellings kreeping through the korpus
Of kontemporary lingo like an illness someone someday
(The trespass of metaphor) is going to spell "kancer."

True, there have been recidivists in opposite
Direction (a falling away perhaps from the Platonic ideal
Of *tò kalón**) like "calisthenics" and Maria Callas,
Who seem to have preferred the less marblelike romance
Of traditional English. This and related factors make all
Supporters of the letter "k" in legitimate forms
And avatars cherish it with fiery intensity—
All the more when besieged by forces beyond
Anyone's control, at least, with social or medical
Remedies now available. Dr. Kaposi named it,
That sarcoma earmarking a mortal syndrome thus far

* *tò kalón:* Greek, "the beautiful"

Incurable and spreading overland like acid rain.
A sense of helplessness is not in the repertory
Of our national consciousness, we have no aptitude
For standing by as chill winds rise, the shadows gather,
And gray light glides into the room where a seated figure
Has taken up his post by the window, facing away from us,
No longer bothering to speak, his mind at one with whatever
Is beyond the ordinary spell of language, whatever dreams us
Into that placeless place, its nearest image a cloudless
Sky at dusk, just before the slow ascent of the moon.

LA MADELEINE

1.

Posters of Juliette Greco, the Eiffel
Tower. A good French bistro in the Village,
Its cuisine by some oversight not yet
Widely known; all the more murmured over
By our party of four avid diners,
Leaning forward over the red-checked cloth.
First course dispatched in record time, I could
Be more deliberate with the second,
Enough to admire each tender forkful
Of the fragrant *Coquille St. Jacques,* steaming
In its ribbed scallop shell—eyes even so
Straying to glance at plates on either side.
In fact, we all sampled each other's entrée
And, satisfied, returned to our first choice.
When time came to moan at the dessert list,
Among the dazzlements our friend Richard,
The translator of Proust, saw handwritten
Copperplate flourishes near the bottom
Propose "Compote de Fraises avec Madeleines."
In lieu of some duller, full-dress homage,
We had them brought for all of us, berries
In red syrup, plus moist, butter-and-egg
Cakes, fluted backs golden by candlelight.
Why *don't* they call these little scallop shells
"Les biscuits St. Jacques"? No, another more
Romantic saint has given them her name.
(Mary Magdalene's the revered object
Of pilgrimages as well, her grotto
In Provence—but let's postpone that visit.)

                        My story over coffee
Began with a concert given at La Madeleine,
The church disguised as a svelte Greek temple,

Where Parisians rich or devout or both at once
Come to see and be seen or, who knows, seek
Forgiveness for sins like self-righteousness.
Still queasy from a three-hour lunch, never mind,
I'd bought my ticket, let music be the tonic
For day-of-arrival hyperactivity. . . .
Ushers were all women of the congregation,
Older, *soignées,* managing subtly to convey
The impression that each was the finer, calmer
Outcome of a worldly personal history now
Put aside in favor of good works and some ideal
Of repose. The one who seated me, gray silk jacket
Over pleated mauve *charmeuse,* smiled and gravely
Searched my eyes as I did hers, both of us refreshed,
I think, poised at ready for an hour of colliding
Gold reverberations, courtesy of Gabrieli. . . .
A week later in a ward of the American Hospital
I saw that same devout double of Jeanne Moreau
Making what looked like a round of volunteer
Visits to the dying—one of them a friend
I'd come to see. The image surviving, framed
Against starched white bedclothes, is a dark profile
Bent slightly forward as she takes the elderly,
Mottled hand of a patient, his health now broken,
Yet only a year ago young and strong and immune.

2.

Proust would have been a flâneur in La Madeleine,
Along with how many prototypes of Odette de Crécy.
And what did he know about its patroness?
A few paintings from the Louvre or Venice,
Namesake heroines in Balzac and Fromentin,
Plus his own in the story *L'Indifférent.* . . . I
Remember from a visit to Galilee (four years

Now) on our drive north along the bluegreen lake,
A signpost marked MIGDAL (in Hebrew: "tower").
That must have been, seventy generations back,
The place of origin of Saint Mary, Jesus' friend,
The only woman that might count as a disciple
And first to recognize, according to Saint John,
Her risen Lord. Whether as well the suppliant
Who wept at Jesus' feet and dried them with her hair,
Sumptuous, "a great sinner," with gold to spend
For an alabaster vase of fragrant spikenard—
Well, tradition's the richer for having thought so.
Because of their devotion, Mary of Magdala
And the Beloved Disciple in time emerged
As closest to his heart—with iconic appeal as well,
To judge by Renaissance art and its aftermath.
"Let him who is without sin cast the first stone at her."
Weakness of the flesh was routine, so decreed
The late Church fathers as the taxonomy
Of transgression was being drafted. Witness
Paolo and Francesca, lovers whose misdeed
Weighed just enough to earn them a fiery nest
At the whirlwind's heart in upper Inferno—
And perpetual fame in the Testament of Beauty.

3.

You were one of those four at dinner, remember?
Any candlelit meal by extension also serves
To celebrate years of settled union. The lens
Of the mind's eye is I guess appropriately
Vaselined by time so that scenes from the life
Return in a tender, peach-toned soft-focus.
Happy years? Yes, at first. Afterwards, four or five
Spent *together* at least, trying to remember
Happiness is only one kind of fulfillment.

A riddle to imagine how you see us now—
But then, I never knew, not even in the early days,
Before you came to see larks and sparks (Parents,
Avoid them) as betrayal pure and simple.
Thinking of you intent on *Pelléas* (Act III:
Mélisande leans from a tower window and lets
Yards of golden hair cascade over her lover),
Your right hand aloft and darting, to assist
The maestro; or tickled by a page in Colette;
Or quoting an Auden line that seemed to hold
All wisdom, who wouldn't assume words and music
Had some point for you in mere experience,
Were more than self-enclosed palaces of art,
In fact, offered shelter and counsel even to us
With our grouches, gourmandise, and dirty socks?
No? On conduct taken for granted in Bloomsbury
Or Montmartre down came a gavel termed *Love*.
The daze of seeing you doubt I did, the jolt
Of hearing instinct or impulse interpreted
As callousness aforethought—one more lesson
In the power of words, nothing like clock hands
Unfailingly recycled to the harmless
Hour before what was said was said. . . . Two years along,
I can see, though, that time is absolution, and many
Rehearsals have now sublimed the old debate
Into light breezes like those the opera chorus
Irresistibly wafted into the key of F major,
Or like a barcarolle, a waltz, a cradle song—
"Lay your sleeping head, my love, human. . . ."

4.

Faceless harm, invasions up from the id,
That underworld mined with caverns accessible
Only through the Gate of Horn, or the maudlin

Inarticulation that overflows censorship
When we stretch out for today's analysis
In the position of love and sleep and death.
Where does the violence come from, and who
Is being killed. . . . The undeterred cast a stone,
And another and another, heaping a rubble cairn
Over the buried victim's blood-soaked clothes,
That fossilized taboos, appearances, the will
Of the majority, this time also be enforced.

5.

Those travels in the provinces,
Up mountain to Vézelay;
Or underground in Lascaux
To trace vestiges left
By a social unit clothed
In half-cured pelts of a mammal
Cousin at many removes,
First effort to draw a fine
Distinction between the human
And the animal. Outlines
Of aurochs, stag, and ibex
In soot or manganese
Dredge up iconic imprints
Of internal prehistory—
Attraction and disgust
At the touch of a furred flank,
Perceived at once as foe
And bloodhot, maternal
Source of nourishment.
Would the stag at last forgive us
For bringing him down with a spear,
And send us more of his kind
In seasons to come? Only

If we kept his image alive
In a vault deep underground,
Where he ranged for humid aeons
Among four-legged fellows
At ease in the limestone fields
Enclosing a pitch darkness
Now and then broken when swaying
Torchlights rounded a veer
In the cave (distant, inverse
Forebear of the highrise),
Like a long chain of molten
Gold, to bring new cravings,
Forms, propitiations,
To hallowed flocks already
Portrayed by an earlier art,
Memorial of what's called
(After the cave's first name)
The Magdalenian culture.

A pause here before I forget
(Sympathy for the waiter
With several plates on his arm)
To mention Sainte-Baume, Mary's
Hermitage late in life.
Golden Legend recounts
How with Martha and Lazarus
She sailed to Gaul, arriving
At Roman Marsilia,
Where (the spirit's wings
Widepread) she preached in *koinē*
To listening multitudes
Of stolid barbarians—
And, years after, withdrew
To a hillside cave near Aix,
Her final days told out

In prayerful penitence,
Itself the fragrant balm
Preparing her body for death.
Today's visitor enters
A humid darkness, the rough
Stone floor cratered with puddles
Reflecting liquid shards
Of larkspur blue and scarlet
From stained-glass ogive windows.
In cool silence you may
Say a prayer to the saint,
Rise and find a path
Through trembling, jewel-like water,
Pause at the door to look back—
Then exit into the whitehot
Sun towering over the Midi.

6.

Feast of St. James, 1989

Dear David, Happy fifty-sixth birthday. Shall I
This time write (as I daily think of you)
And allow friendship to go on evolving—
In some ways more evenhanded than back
When you were with us, subject to wincing
Stresses the temple of the body has to bear,
Hunger pangs, noise, fatigue, bronchitis.
The week of your death, along Village sidewalks
Linden flowers dusted the air with the faint
Potpourri that will now always summon up,
In bouts of silent thought, our own *belle époque.* . . .

At any dinner party the best finale was you,
A compote of phrases derived from native wit

And close readings of the Elizabethans,
James, Yeats, Stevens, and *The Remembrance.*
Involuntary allusion smiles and sees you
As a second Charles Swann, relaxed and upright
In a *traghetto* as you skimmed across the Canal
Under the shadow of Santa Maria della Salute
To lend some luster to a gathering where,
Apparently, simply leaning against a door,
Arms folded, face lit by an amused, benign
Expression, could magnetize them to your side,
Eager for smiling urbanity's angle on whatever
Venice might be buzzing about that given day.
You had (outside *Swan Lake*) no single Odette,
Rather, a series, cygnet after black or white
Cygnet, whom with a twinkle you brought to parties
(Depending) or skipped parties to stay home with. . . .
Memory's parenthetical invasions of the daily
Round promise to keep you now and future decades
The faithful companion of my "decrepit age,"
As Yeats ("The Tower") called the rest of his climb.

Venice from time immemorial beset by plagues,
No surprise should the palazzo's proprietress,
Hearing of your condition, panic and with all
The innocence of misinformation have your floor
Fumigated, clouds of tear-gas mingling with those
In the library ceiling's frescoes. . . . When you turned
For a last look at the Barbaro (before the long
"Wreck of body, slow decay of blood"), slimegreen
Waves at work to dissolve how many surrounding
Morose or fanciful façades, over the Mahlerian rush
Of waters and motors, bells tolling from the distant
Campanile, dialect outcries, adagio strings
Wafting across the Canal, was there also, if heard
Only in the inner ear, a faintly beating sibilance,
Descending, settling to rest, the wings of the dove?

7.

LA MADDALENA

The baroque streetwalker Caravaggio painted,
His contemporary, a piece of cake from Trastevere
In Fortuny brocade, slumped in a chair by cast-off
Finery, serpentine chains of massive gold,
A broken string of pearls, vial of fragrant oil
She can no longer pour over the Master's head
And anoint him king. Head bowed, auburn hair
Streaming over her shoulders, behold a type
Of the unfaithful, returned from the fleshpots,
Agonized and with no intimation that dawning
Day in a garden outside the city will find her
Weeping by the tomb ("Elle a pleuré comme
Une Madeleine," as older women used to say),
Only to hear her name and answer, "Rabboni!"
Then be commanded to go and tell the brothers,
Her "I have seen the Lord!" echoing down
Twenty centuries in the breaking of the bread—
Whenever broken "for the remembrance of me."

8.

Feast of St. Mary Magdalene, 1990

Mary of Magdala,
Vividest apostle,
Teach me to be faithful;

And to discount mistakes
Others may have made
Out of pain and confusion.

Pray for the sick, the dying,
And those who watch at their side.
Help us to dry our tears;

Or, if they will not cease,
Then let them bathe the feet
Of our best advocate.

At each new step of the stair,
Blessed Mary, pray for us—
And remember us on that day.

RIGHT AND LEFT HAND

Late dawning of the solstice
Roughs them in in charcoal:
Leafless handtrees with gnarling

At the joints a flexed
Tendon unbends, the trunk
A trellis for swollen veins.

Instruments of love
Or strife, now quilted palm,
Now knuckleheaded fist—

There were times when the ache
To make tracks as a southpaw
Derailed your John Hancock.

Eve's hand in his, Adam
Left obedience behind
(The twined snake flickering

Approval). They ate and knew
What they did. A son was born,
Another: the story's rightful

Heirs. But whose handiwork
Has never charred in the flame
Of a child's silent gaze?

RESOLUTIONS

Alice in winterland—
and everyone else gone to Luxor.
Nights the shop windows
look safe and warm, a gold frame
for silk, for leather; which look good *there,*

but take them home to meet my things?
January windowpanes have in common
a scrim of steam bright droplets
cut through like diamond comets. . . .
Livingroom, you'll go on hazy display

to the apartment opposite until—
until discretion rolls down
one of our blinds. City life
is an education: aboriginal
art in the showrooms; *Carmen* at the Met;

or ask that gray-haired guard at the Modern.
And the rules of new independence?
Meals planned with at least one item
remembered from childhood; an hour
scheduled daily on the telephone;

for Sunday lunch, three friends, staunch, kind,
gifted at what (and not) to say. Safeguards. . . .
Still, when that unknown tenant, shopping
bag in hand, steps into the elevator,
glances a split second, then looks down—

Oh, if being guarded meant the same as being safe.

INFERNAL REGIONS AND
THE INVISIBLE GIRL

(Frances Milton Trollope, the mother of the novelist, was an author in her own right. She arrived in America with three of her children on Christmas Eve in 1827. She settled in Cincinnati a few months later, where, eventually, she built a "Bazaar." It was an emporium for fancy goods, the upper stories reserved for social and cultural events. On her return to England, Mrs. Trollope completed Domestic Manners of the Americans, *published in 1832 to acclaim in England and opprobrium in America. Mary Russell Mitford, novelist and dramatist, author of* Our Village, *was a friend and literary sponsor. The following conversation takes place between them at Harrow, after Mrs. Trollope's return, a time when it's possible to imagine her practicing aloud for her book.)*

Had I the tenth part of your great descriptive
Powers, my dear Miss Mitford. . . . I do not,
Yet I am writing very diligently.
Three years' atrocious discommodity:
The nearest thing of course is Dante, nor
Do you imagine I mean the *Paradiso*.
Lasciate ogni speranza. . . . Yes, precisely.
I felt that I had come to River Styx:
Miasmal waters of the Mississippi,
And crocodiles, the horror, the horror of them!
How one pitied the wretched woodcutter
Who lives in their society on the shore,
Selling fuel to passing steamboats, half
Dead from hunger, burning with ague, whisky
His single remedy and sole distraction. . . .
At first the town of Cincinnati seemed
A different prospect, built of brick and stone—
The site is truly splendid, hills and slopes
That overlook the beautiful Ohio.
Even so, I ought to have foreseen
An outpost in the American wilds, not forty
Years old, could hardly produce amenities
Comparable to those of Bath or Malvern.

Its citizens are far outnumbered by
Their roving pigs, who swarm the streets and act
As unpaid rubbish carters, for there are
No others to perform that service. Of course,
Like most new towns, it's based on commerce, not
On ancient feudal privilege and custom.
Still, I maintain that manners cost us nothing,
That a gentlewoman travelling
With her children and no husband there
To assist her might in reason hope to have
Kindly treatment from all but crocodiles.
As she was English she could count on nothing
Of the sort! How they loathe their mother
Country and all its works! Fanatical
Patriotism. . . . Also, I was female,
Therefore had broken hallowed rules of conduct
Merely by refusing to stay at home.
A seven-fold shield of insignificance
Guards American womanhood from the least
Stain of independent activity.
The Yankee disposes; his wife and chattels obey.
He also chews tobacco, and he spits
Whether provoked or not—Miss Mitford, we
Laugh, but it is revolting, you can't conceive—.
And then, a *total* lack of probity
Where interest is concerned, which might, believe me,
Set canny Yorkshire at defiance. Money
Tops the range of Yankee aspiration.
My wish to show them other modes of life
Overrode natural caution. Would they
Ever have attained the realms where I
Proposed to take them? Ah, it cost me dearly
To leave my marvelous Bazaar so soon
After building it. A charming resort,
Egypto-Graeco-Moresco-Gothic, the style—

Byronic, one might say, or like the Regent's
Pavilion. Commerce on the street level,
And all of painting, music, and poetry
I could arrange for on the floors above:
A slow ascent to Heaven, as in Dante.
In fact, they had their own *Inferno*—surely
I mentioned meeting a Frenchman named Dorfeuille?
Disheartened, but very nice. His Western Museum
Had not done well. Geology and fossils,
Though most instructive, brought few visitors.
Some novelties and freaks of nature fared
Little better. No, his greatest triumph
Was our "Infernal Regions," devised with help
From a young sculptor—Hiram Powers, very
Gifted. The figures, formed, alas, in wax,
Were nonetheless extremely fine. Ha-*ha*,
They gave the spectators a terrible fright,
And that experience was much enjoyed.
Hell is the core of their religious faith,
You see. I heard a three-hour Baptist sermon
On the dread topic, worse by far than our
Infernal Regions. "Revivals," so they're called,
Provide the summer entertainment, and—
I shan't forbear to say—are vile occasions
Indeed, a base infection of irreligion.
It shall be called a heinous libel, yet
I tell you that young *ladies* put themselves
In fits of madness—answering the divine
Afflatus (they believe). They rush headlong
To the great altar, fling themselves to earth,
And then the groans, the tears, the flailing limbs,
The shrieked and inarticulate confessions—.
More than one young person's neck I saw
Encircled by a reverend arm, as he bent
Forward and whispered like the toad at Eve's

Ear. . . . A shocking spectacle, but then
Infernality's the key to Yankee
Affective life, for it reminds them of home;
And anyone who had the skill to give
Visible form to such imaginations
Was sure to draw the multitudes. These thoughts
I represented to Monsieur Dorfeuille.
I made his fortune! Not my own, I fear.
The difficulties were immense, children
Ill, my dear husband far away, unable
To comfort. . . . That second year I too was stricken.
Nine weeks I could not leave my room. The novels
Of Mr. Cooper occupied my hours—
You've read them? I never closed my eyes but saw
Myriads of bloody scalps afloat in my dreams. . . .
Red Indians crept about with noiseless tread;
Forests blazed; whichever way I fled
A keen eye and a long rifle were sure
To be on my trail. . . . But I eluded them
And have survived. Ah, here's my son! Henry,
Come and greet our guest. He was my mainstay
In America, Miss Mitford. And—
Shall I tell this? Of course I shall. You see,
"Infernal Regions" was not the first tableau
That I devised for our good friend's Museum.
The old Egyptian Mysteries have always
Held a fascination for me, thus
I wondered whether we might not set up
A secret oracle in a magic chamber. . . .
But not for gawking eyes. Instead, the voice
Of a girl, invisible but near at hand
To answer any question posed (provided
It was proper, of course). They came in droves
To consult this prodigy, and some believed.
Her answers came in Latin, French, and Greek,

Striking wonder into the hearts of all—
Much as the poet reveres his sacred Muse.
No, Miss Mitford, the oracle was not
Myself, I have no Greek nor Latin, only
A little French. It was my boy, my Henry.
He was so young his treble voice could be
Mistaken for a girl's. Concealed in the gloom
Of the Magic Chamber, he replied to all
Their questions—very sagely, may I say.
Advice in Greek was listened to with hushed
Respect, however little understood.
They hearkened to *invisibility*—
A source of truth not readily confuted—
But never once to me! Perhaps, when I
Myself have put on invisibility,
Speaking to them from print on page, they shall?

COVENTRY

Even if not sent there, some would go
just to visit a byword for banishment, or
nod and smile at Tudor cottages
verifying their age among highways
athrottle with the local Jaguar—
nine centuries ago the route of (do
they know for certain?) Godiva's midday ride
through narrow, cobbled streets. Still there, and nude,
a statue on a civic pedestal,
she serves as patron for the recent mall.

St. Michael's ruin has no plans to recover
from the blitzkrieg fires of 1940,
visibly content with its roof of sky,
a brownstone sheepfold with fence of ogives,
tracery drained of blood-red or river-
blue glass. A few steps north, in autumn sun,
the adjunct modernist cathedral proves
by inscription that Britten's sharp baton
rode lightly above the *War Requiem*
as, borrowing the tenor of Peter Pears,

Wilfred Owen back from the fields of France
grafted his words onto the older hymn
under the eyes of a merciful giant.
The clash of arms turned music of the spheres
to counteract a deadly expedient
how many thousands now cannot denounce.
Black swallows rise and circle as bells chime
the congregants inside at Evensong,
as if war'd been a roughhewn cornerstone
in the edifice of Common Market peace.

Et lux perpetua luceat eis:
Owen, Britten, Pears, all three moved out

of earshot to that other Coventry,
attendants of the blessed lady, prompted
perhaps by music's blinding insights. Is it
because an icon forfeits all privacy
that every bystander at last is tempted,
eye at keyhole or shutter?—this means you,
Peeping Tom, and I, and you, and you, oh,
on fire to see the last thing we will ever see.

SOMERSET ALCAICS

East Coker: sun afire in midwinter, rain-of-gold
Teardrops at tip of holly and ivy leaf
        Instills nativity. (A warm day
    Travellers had of it down from Wells to

St. Michael's Church, where T.S.E.'s ancestors
Once bowed their heads then sailed for "Jerusalem.")
        Scion, return and nest your ashes
    Here in the wall at the door they left by.

Low barrel vault with crossbeams of oak painted
Black. Norman belfry. Greenest of churchyards. And
        Still, "In my end is my beginning"?
    Pray for the souls of the antisemites.

                                    Christmas, 1987

AFTER RILKE

You, God, my next-door neighbor, how many times
Whole nights I knocked and knocked to wake you.
Yet rarely do I hear you so much as breathe;
Then guess: you're by yourself in the livingroom.
Yet, if you needed something, no one's there—
You know, to pour a glass of wine for you to taste.
One servant waits, at least. Just make a sign.
I'm right here, a step away.

For no real reason a single panel, paper-thin,
Stands between us. One word from you, though
(Or even from me), and that wood,
Ah, breaks through—
Soundlessly, with no crash or cry.

THE JAUNT

In party outfits, two by two or one by one
(I was expected to go along as well),
They step up the steep gangplank, hands on
Metal railing. The river, youthful also
In midnight blue with sunset-tinted wavelets,
Lets them borrow its broad back
For an evening's unhurried round trip,
Which won't interrupt old river habits for long.
Not the chop and churn of big propellers
As the rocking stern heaves off and wheels fanwise
Into the current, nor a short blast from the stack,
Not the up-tempo drumbeat of the black-tie combo
Nor an answering fusillade of popped corks, not geysers
Of laughter pitched flagpole high among flailing
Limbs out on the polished floor nor the mixed
Babble of sideline comment over bubbling glasses
Can shake that seamless imperturbability. . . .

When the springy net of sparkles has shrunk and faded
Out of sight, the last rough throb been coaxed
From the tenor sax's frog-in-the-throat, the final
Needling tremolo of the clarinet been wrapped up
In distance, suddenly it is strange to be here
In lilac afterglow with trout-leap and mayfly. . . .
Strange, too, how our part of the river continues
To trundle along its tonnages of water and motion.

The unused ticket spins to the ground.
As much as any person not two people can
I miss the jaunt, for just this one hour of dusk. . . .
Then, a veiled echo, my name called as I turn
To answer, eyes adjusting to where we are
At the pivot of night, the cusp of light.
Light enough to feel our way back to the grove
Of alders along the curving path beside the river;
Light enough to recognize my life when I see it,
Going in its direction, more or less at the same pace.

1992

〉 〉

for Christopher Corwin

1.

1949

I took the water she gave me, a dark young woman
in a "Spanish," off the shoulder, ruffled blouse—
a cover girl, almost (like the maiden on the Sun-
Maid raisin box), remembering to smile for tourist
cameras, a bright "wine-stain" birthmark
on her arm prominent as she calmly
ladled draughts from *The Fountain of Youth*
into a paper cup, whose contents ignited
in noonday light. This was St. Augustine,
Florida, summer I was six going on seven.
Too young to see the paradox, I drank; and waited
for legendary water to transform my life.

The town boasted its fort from the Golden Century,
turreted, built of tabby, and "the oldest schoolhouse
in the United States." A steady stream of visitors
kept things lively, half to see the monuments, half
to turn a tone darker; and there was always
the barely reined-in surge of tropic leaves and flowers.
Ponce de León's public-relations name for the land
had in a sense come true, and these middle-aged
vacationers rediscovering their bodies
found a source mazes of cypress swamp
and jaws of the dragon had kept from him.

(I'll say our server was Dolores Curtis,
a Tampa native, 23. Day's work done,
she walks to her apartment, a new Spanish
mission stucco, tiled in red terracotta.
The small white Zenith radio crackles
a broadcast speech of Harry Truman's.
Station break, static, a cigarette ad,
followed by Glenn Miller. Off comes the peasant

costume, panties, bra; on comes the shower.
A String of Pearls. . . . Bright drops spill
on white, honeycomb-patterned tiles
as she swaddles the towel into a turban,
pink hibiscus nodding outside the window,
the blood-red stamens dusted gold with pollen.

By 6:30 Wayne's driven up in his green Packard.
A "shave-and-a-haircut" knock on the door. "Two bits,"
she says as she lets in his 100-watt smile,
fending him off, a little. Where to? The Shangri-La
Drive-In, famous for shrimp, fries, and Schlitz.

Afterwards they drive to the beach and park.
Lucky Tiger tonic slicking his pompadour
in place fails to hold as he takes a movie pose
over her. August heat and damp, a single mosquito
keening around them. She lets him go just so
far, not a step more until they're married.
Wayne works for his daddy, owner of five hundred
acres of citrus out from East Palatka, plus
some swamp acquired during the Florida Bubble.
He's supposed to make his own way, though,
and hasn't saved enough for down payment
on a house, not yet. A deep kiss, and it's too
far, as waves crash and collapse, foam races
along the shore, salt fragrance, the fountain of youth.)

My first journey anywhere. Ragged silhouette
of distant palms, percussive sun, and,
farther out, beach grass and low shrubs that dot
the rolling dunes, dimpled swells of sand gliding
down to the brushed cymbals of an old Atlantic
whose unhindered horizon and somersaulting waves
left me dazed, thirsty, and blinking. The sunstarred

heft of the tide built and rebuilt its seagreen
redundant thunderheads to the steady roar
and quick applause of invisible crowds. A sand
castle modeled on their Spanish prototype
took form at the edge as I patted grainy
mortar into place and shaped a turret, only
to have it erased, along with my childishly
scrawled name, while the *perpetuum mobile*
waves slung their white lassoes higher and higher. . . .

All of this as we half-orphans put out tendrils
toward our new mother, twelve years Daddy's junior.
Herself a World War widow at 25, she was "brunette,"
stylish, affectionate, and liked to laugh.
Youngest of the children and the first,
in trustful desperation, to call her "Mama,"
I knew already *something* was wrong with me.
Missing a scented, nervous warmth since my second birthday,
I was fearful of everything—of transgression
and the punishment that followed, of going
to unfamiliar places, meeting strangers there.
Even now I dread these unmasked statements,
their therapeutic slant and trust in fact,
failure to scan or use productive rhyme
or metaphor. Yet can't deny the will to
set out in search of what it is that shaped
one witness's imagining of time
(five late-20th century decades sifting
numbered moments through the infinity
sign's tipped hourglass) and make available
the content of the world that is my case—
composed in part by all those I have met,
thinking through the story of who we are.

2.

1971

"C.C. Rider, see what you have done . . ." came over
the car radio from some station west of Twin Falls,
Idaho, where Ann and I'd quarreled through a restless
night in early June, in fact, had been on edge
half the drive through Wyoming (travel's downside
tendency to fray good humor). Here we were
on the road again, to spend a second summer
with her mother in Oregon, a chance to look
closer at things a first encounter only part-way
comprehended. . . . And last night? A few too many
shots on the rocks, one delayed result,
that driving felt queasy as the Rambler
hugged hairpin curves of a state highway roughly
paralleling whitewater rapids of the Snake.
A quick sarcasm, and we picked up (eagerly?)
the argument where midnight had left it.
Car and wheel close to blind rage, for safety's
sake I pulled off the road, fifteen miles
south of Boise. Unbroken expanse of pale
blue sky; far pastures; leaning fencepost
overgrown with wild sweetpea, the summer bees'
resort. Attention bent to that particular
fragrant hum, which I stabbingly
perceived as a nectared résumé of our best
moments. "Do we call it off then?" Anyone
could tell more was meant than the quarrel,
or why so loud a heartbeat in my ears?
Once-in-a-lifetime glances exchanged.
Solemn nod, blinking eyes. Then an hour of silence.
Almost to the day, one slowly grinding year
later, sharp legal instruments set us apart. . . .

How much plot unfolds on our highways,
the routine vehicular habit, cradle to grave

In Conestoga style, self-contained movable
houses like the small silver one we saw
sail past us that morning, a single driver
at the wheel of the Chevy hauling it.

(He wondered who they were, those two parked
roadside out there in the lap of nowhere.
Mike Kovich, 36, of The Dalles, Oregon,
on the loose and in transit after the splitup.
Connie—his ex—got the house but told him
to keep his stupid trailer. She plans to stay
in Salt Lake City, on 9th Street, a view
of the Wasatch Mountains to the east and, opposite,
the Angel Moroni atop the Temple spire. In time,
of course, you stop seeing any view. Her job
with Prudential takes up the daylight hours,
besides which, she has a little girl to raise.

When Mike told her he was leaving, she cried—
more for Amber's having to grow up without a father
than anything else. He wanted her to break the news.
Amber was already down with a cold, and it just
seemed really mean. She saw red and realized
she'd clobber anyone who tried to hurt her child,
then thought, Wait, this is how people go off
the deep end. Mike hadn't been himself a couple
of years now, he missed his buddies back
in The Dalles. A lot of Vietnam vets are moody,
it said in *Family Circle*. He wouldn't even
watch TV with her, just sat in the den and fiddled
with his rod and tackle or read through beatup
back issues of *Field and Stream*.
They'd stopped making love, naturally, and some
nights Mike would get in late, smelling of booze.
OK, he didn't like his job with the power company,
but why take it out on her? She's embarrassed

at being a divorcée, and just might remarry if
somebody decent who doesn't mind she's already
got a kid shows up and asks her the right way.
But like, she's nothing special, really. It would
take a bighearted kind of guy even to notice her,
and frankly there just aren't that many around.

Mike feels bad about leaving and knows he has
hurt his little daughter. If he had it to do
over again, maybe he'd have stayed and given
the hell up like everybody else. Just that,
nighttimes, when you wake up and begin to see
white water shunting over the rocks, a tall stand
of Engelmann spruce above. . . . You cast and recast,
the little speckled fly dancing from wavecrest
to crest, Jay (who'd been their best man) fifty
yards upriver, likewise, in a different rhythm.
Six-packs nest in the cooler, a hawk balances
on an updraft, the air-conditioning pouring out
of the woods is a green ballad, and the one life
you get on earth tastes good. . . . What he doesn't
know yet is that, when he gets there and starts
asking, they'll tell him Jay's gone to Montana,
went to see a friend who lives on Flathead Lake,
without so much as goodbye or Please Forward.)

3.

1988
Seventeen years—enough time for the child we
never had to be enrolling at Reed or Yale—elapsed
before I passed that way again, Sandy intent
on the road, our course set in the opposite
direction this trip. We'd spent several mild
days in Seattle before crossing Lake Washington
to pick up I-90 East; from there, on to the black
peaks, snowcapped even in June, of the Wenatchee Range.
A steady glide down to arid plains, a bridge
over the Columbia, tracking the sun southward
as it pounded on the anvil of the desert all
the way to Idaho. Smiling goodbye that morning,
the friend we'd stayed with had handed us
a dozen Granny Smiths for the road, possibly
to suggest that the best apples put an edge
of tartness on the sweet to make it carry.
Sunlight played around the car interior
as my Swiss Army knife cut green and white
slices for the driver, worker's compensation
for rigors of the road. He seemed mollified,
that day, at least. At best. Nine months
and several flareups later we parted. For which
I accept responsibility—putting this forward,
in fact, as one more installment in response.
Both plaintiffs had their points. Were we
like stags, antlers tangled, an inextricable
deadlock bound to end in dual extinction?
"One to One," the poem written a decade
earlier termed it, with no results outside
the words themselves, a reconciled lament. Partly
reconciled—and the distant background for that
morning, afternoon and evening as we matched
itineraries with the river, then, at sunset,
pulled off to find a Day's Inn in Twin Falls.

(Cal Svenborg switches on the lights
in the 7-11, goes around checking stock
in the gray fluorescent light. The last day
before vacation. He'll go upstate to Moscow
and visit his mother, who's been diagnosed
with Parkinson's. Question is whether to take
Theresa with him. Mother won't like her,
which, if he'd stopped to think about it,
he could have figured out when they met
two months ago at the Demolition Derby.
He thinks about last night over at her place,
lace on the pillow shams and a big Elvis
on velvet hanging in the livingroom.
She lit a red candle that smelled like roses,
then played a video while she gave him a neck rub.
They each cracked open a Coors, and she
talked about growing up in North Dakota,
on "the Res," as she called it, how her dad
got shot the weekend before graduation.
Her mother just caved in and she had to
take over. Nuns kept trying to smother her.
"I'm sure glad that's over with," but something
in her voice made him look up. She was crying.
It felt sad, like, you know, when you're maybe
driving by yourself somewhere and you wonder
if your life really amounts to anything.
Her soft brown hair was fluffed out,
she was a little sunburned and said ouch when
he touched her. Later, when she looked up at him
and asked if he thought they were too young
to get married, he shook his head, and she laughed. . . .
He turns on the radio and it's the middle
of a song he likes by the Dead Milkmen,
can't remember the name. Wait. He hears
something scuttling around in the back room.
Opens the door and as the light goes on,

sees two scared eyes flashing at him and then
gray and black-striped fur dash behind
a stack of cartons. Shit, a raccoon, how did *that*
get in here? He notices the window's open,
right next to a tree branch. Up front
the buzzer buzzes as the first customer
of the day comes in. And there goes the raccoon
out the window, born free again, a ripped
open box of Cracker Jacks left behind.)

1956

By car with my parents that August to Atlanta:
a dazzled gaze at freeways and tall buildings,
not to mention hills and valleys—novelties
to one from the flatlands farther south.
Here was Peachtree Street, department stores,
taxis, blinking marquees, and out by Ponce de Leon
Drive, the huge '20s-Moorish Fox Theater, vast
as any mosque in Istanbul. Or the Greek Revival,
Tara-like mansions of Buckhead. We stayed
with relatives in one, high up on a shady hill
at the end of a precipitous driveway.
Much less than that would have impressed. Home
could be a castle? And talk, guarded interest
in a president who regularly flew down
for relaxation on the Augusta golf links;
along with sharply drawled regret
for the Supreme Court decree that separate
wasn't equal. Legislative wheels
heaved into motion to haul away a sleepy
self-styled agrarianism and its rougher urban
counterpart, old Doric columns and tin-roofed
shacks alike leveled and Gone with the Wind. . . .

I was taken to the Cyclorama, an in-the-round
epic painting of the Battle of Atlanta,
shading insensibly into three-D dioramas
with dead mannequin soldiers sprawled on red
clay dyed darker red by gallons of spilled
stage blood, emblem for the cost of a war
fought when the Southern states filed for divorce.
Slavery was evil, I knew as soon as I could think.
And tried to keep secret my failure to feel "above"
the everyday people nice people termed colored
so as to avoid a slur gubernatorial hopefuls

often brandished from the courthouse steps.
Reunion is never quite the same as Union,
but has a tang of its own almost as well known.

(Rosetta Haines, employed at Emory Hospital,
had a forty-fifth birthday last week. Her sister,
who works for a family in Buckhead, and several
of her friends gave her a nice party—Lord knows
she's got blessings to count. What she doesn't
have's a special girlfriend right now, not since
Yvonne left six months ago. Vonnie was young still,
hadn't made up her mind what she wanted, and
whether she ought to have her baby boy raised
by two womenfolk, see—but may yet come back
to this little house in Buttermilk Bottom.
It's kept up nice, even got a new Magnavox
paid for on installment plan. A big change
from the old place outside of Columbus, now *that*
was hard. No electric, no plumbing, no heat.
You boiled laundry in a big black three-legged pot
out back of the house those hot July mornings,
standing in the shade of the chinaberry tree.
House sat up on brick pilings, high enough
for children to crawl under and look for doodlebugs.
Half the yard covered in kudzu vine, and Mama
had her cans of petunias and snow-on-the-mountain
on the front porch, where she'd sit Sunday evening,
a little can of Tuberose handy. Father passed,
and she's still there, not able for much,
arthritis got to her hands, but she still cleans
the Church of the Nazarenes weekly,
walks a mile there every Friday afternoon—
Lysol, a sponge, a mop, Freewax—and gets by.

Lot better deal to live in Atlanta
with a steady job and a pension plan. Ten years

she's been taking care of the sick at Emory Hospital,
emptying their bedpans, giving them sponge baths, listening
to their stories, and saying, Don't worry, your children
are sure coming to visit today. But when they haven't,
saying, Now, don't fret, they'll come tomorrow.

She slips on her glasses and listens to the news.
It covers over the way she misses Yvonne.
On the bureau is a jar of Artra. She gets up,
unscrews the lid, and starts to rub her arms with it.
News goes to people picketing a school,
knocked down by firehoses, attack dogs unleashed—
would you believe that? She listens and frowns.
Looks down at her hands, the jar in them,
its label, the brightly colored promotions.
Tosses it aside and snaps off the TV.
An image of a public drinking fountain
marked "White Only" rises in her mind. . . .
On the window sill a line of purple African
violets Mama gave her. Probably thirsty.
She waters them, careful not to wet the delicate,
peach-fuzz leaves. Somebody frying bacon next door.)

5.

1988

That trek from Florida to California
in early March comes back with a flood
of orange blossom drenching the late air,
starting from Orlando, then a catfish dinner
ten miles outside Tallahassee. Why shouldn't
bedtime at the Palmetto Motel catch me
looking through the dark glass of a Gideon Bible
left in the bureau drawer: "When I was a child,
I spake as a child." And still dream as one,
to judge by the night's dim replay of our old
house, scene of a lifetime supply of drama.

Next day as we left the Florida panhandle
uprushing blue-black clouds burst like giant
piñatas. Warm torrents sheeting down, a frenzied
dance of twilit leaves, the windshield
drunk with wobbling water. Just as abruptly
it was over, seemed never to have happened.
Like a curtain going up, the sky cleared, sun
applied malleable gold foil to bay waters,
pounding it thin as light, the surface
crinkling outward to the Gulf. Four lanes
of the Jubilee Parkway smoothly spanned
an estuary the Mobile River expanded into.
In a hazed distance domes, drums, and refinery
smokestacks compromised the mood a sunset
approach to coastal cities is meant
to stir. Mobile, a naturalistic sprawl down
at the toe of Alabama, dipping into coastal
waters, the name calling to mind as well
those aerial balancing performances
of Alexander Calder, primary colors
suspended on graceful strings and booms

in vibrant constellation. Giving up entire
control allowed his result to evade
the melancholy catatonia sculpture
suffers from among so many living observers
who gather around it to admire and pity.
Of ten thousand configurations possible,
which one did he most intend? One and all,
transformal icons of change—a theory
our Sky Hawk and all its multicolored
coevals spinning along the interstates
might also recall as fluid instances
of spontaneous automobility.
It would have been a contradiction
for us to stop—in fact, a friend in Gulfport
was waiting dinner for us. When we drove up
to his house lazily situated under a live oak
hung with Spanish moss, he came shyly out
on the old veranda and gestured us in.

(Off the highway west of Pascagoula Ray LaNoue
of Biloxi wipes his hands on a Big Boy napkin
after his afternoon snack. This is the last
day of the Tennessee-Arkansas run. He shouldn't
have eaten so much. But driving makes you hungry.
Be a while before supper yet. This weight thing
didn't used to be a problem. What do you
have without your health? Like Daddy: Cancer.
The man's dying. They already went through it
with Diane's father, six months of hospital care.
We all have to go some time, but back when,
you never would have thought the man could
even get sick, let alone—. Everybody said
he was the best foreman Gulf Oil ever had,
strong as a dray horse, six foot one, a veteran.
Times they'd go to the beach, Daddy'd ride

him on his shoulders, like on the top
of the world. Once the whole family
all got dressed up in Sunday clothes
and drove over to that old house—or
museum nowadays—where Jefferson Davis,
President of the Confederate States
of America, once lived. Right on the water
with a big shade porch all around it.
Daddy said you should know something
about your heritage. LaNoues had been
in Mississippi since before the War
Between the States. Cajuns and Irish.

Late sunlight filters through pine needles,
lights up the spread fans of palmettoes still
damp from the rain. A big pair of pink
foam dice hang from the rear-view.
Blue and white books of sales orders
stacked up in the backseat, underneath
a rack of clothes. Weed killer and the lawn-
edger Diane said she wanted he got wholesale
in Chattanooga. A bag of salt-water taffy
for the kids, like the kind Daddy used
to buy for them at the beach. The Escort's
a little overloaded today, and probably
needs an oil change. He thinks about Diane,
about how they've kind of drifted apart,
with all she has to do being a mother. Sometimes
they look at each other, guilty. And then change
the subject. He knows she cares about him, she's
been a big help with Daddy. Cancer. The man's dying.)

6.

1965

I had spent my last rebellious summer
home and boarded the Atlantic Coast Line
for New York, a jolting overnight trip
scored for Carolina voices, darkness,
careening trapezoids of light, stench
of cigars, the random, avant-garde ballet
of travelers shoving into the aisles, one
by one flinging bags into overhead racks
before settling suspiciously next
the studious type buried in his paperback.
How often do twenty-two years have the knack
of knowing when they are afraid? To myself
I seemed all adult confidence, thrilled at being
sprung from the boredom of the southern suburbs.
An abandoned *Wall Street Journal* picked up
and scanned hungrily yielded facts,
figures, but nothing comprehensible,
its print, viewed through ever heavier eyelids,
scattering like army ants into oblivion. . . .
"Wil-ming-ton," the conductor crooned.
"All passengers for Wilmington, Dela-wa-are."
Inkblue late August dawn came to birth,
then shafts of sun on a gliding
panorama of brick and dusty ailanthus trees.
My heart beat on impatience, eyes glancing
over shoulders at essays in *Time*
re Johnson's escalation of the Kennedy
hard-line approach in Vietnam, still unaware
I should concern myself with public policies
that would change my life and everything I knew.

(Isabel Ramos of Cobble Hill, Brooklyn,
pulls her dance clothes out of the locker,

spits at a twelfth-grader who cops a feel,
slams the metal door and runs down the hall,
floorboards scuffed but gleaming like those
in the dance studio on 14th Street in the City.
Forty minutes later she is there at the barre
in a black leotard, bent over forehead to knee.
Ever since she saw José Greco she knew
she would be a dancer. She watches herself
in the mirror, long thin arms joined over
her head, a muscular leg straight out sidewise.
The teacher comes over, corrects her extensions,
and pipes encouragement. A warped LP spins
on a little portable, piano music at a slow
tempo interrupted by brief showers of high
sparkling notes, like a summer fountain.
Outside, early snow falls, parked cars
snug under a blanket of it, the muffled rush
of traffic and an occasional sour horn.
She sees all the girls' reflections
turning around her own in silver-gray light,
the thin bodies, long necks, hair pinned up.
Class over, she gives the teacher five dollars,
gets dressed—boots, overcoat, mittens—
and goes out into the snow. On the F train
a man squeezes up next to her. For a moment
she lets him do it, her eyes on a poster
advertising the World's Fair, then a memory
of those times with her father creeps up,
she smells his breath, feels a rush of nausea,
and pushes out the door, a station too early.
On the platform, a crushed Oreo cookie
someone dropped and someone else stepped on.

She trudges up the stairs, her thighs tired
from the class. Bergen Street, *Iglesia Cristiana*

Manantial de Vida. She crosses herself.
In the hallway, the bang-crash and brass blare
of somebody's radio, *Mi corazón que muere.* . . .
When she opens the door, there is Mama
at the table with a glass of wine, reading
Vanidades. Outside, a brick wall seen
through curtains of falling snow. Since Papa died
in an accident last March—was he drinking
or was the girder slippery with ice?—
it's how Mama spends her evenings. Company
insurance covered it, so Mama gave up her job
at the doll factory and just stays home.
But now, all this wine. In the next room,
Joselito is crying. Isabel says nothing,
goes to him, and picks him up. When she comes back
Mama is flipping through her English textbook.
She looks up, eyes red and teary, says,
"I'm glad you're getting an education.")

7

1973

Julys, every New Yorker tries to make a getaway.
David had given me directions for the three-hour
drive to the little port on Fisher's Island Sound
where he was spending the summer. I knew nothing
about the Nutmeg State, presumably a stretch of mere
connective tissue between the big flank cuts
of New York and Massachusetts. Stonington
was a pause, if only for its odd blend
of leisure and work, ruling class and Portuguese
Americans juxtaposed waterside for contrasting,
overlapping reasons related to salt water.

Whistler's birthplace. A lighthouse museum
where blue-and-white imported by clipper
ships in the China trade vied with whale
tusks webbed over in spidery scrimshaw,
or ancient astrolabes and sextants.
The play of bellied canvas out on the blue,
Watch Hill to one side, Mystic the other,
the sprawl of towels and Coppertoned bodies
on the little manmade beach next a breakwater
fringed with seaweed—how casual and calmly
selected it seemed. David was installed
on Water Street, an address I knew from a book
of the same name, the laureate owner away
in Greece. That his present tenant had the friendship
of poets was only one of his qualities:
his graying Julius Caesar cut; his chortle;
tact—and willingness to read new pages
brought to him as though they might also
be poems earned a gratitude based more
on what he said than what he must have thought.

Top floor, on a sundeck of weathered planking
(walking barefoot on which I later picked up
a couple of splinters), a deadpan bust
of the Emperor Otho presided over deck chairs
and a trough of succulents, as magnums of Callas
hosed from the upstairs speakers. The weekend's
best joke, eclipsing a dozen well-phrased
others, was to slip a pair of sporty shades
over the blank marble eyes of that Roman face.
Over drinks up there, David would read favorite
passages from Firbank or Bishop, the sunset
a huge agate of bruised gold over the horizon,
gull cries mixing with clanks from a distant buoy,
the listener basking in his good luck and only
by moments wondering how on earth to justify it.

(In Old Lyme, Mathilda Howe Vallabriga sorts
the morning mail, pleased when a bright Spanish
stamp appears in the pile. From Luís's cousin
Teresa, with congratulations on her sixtieth. . . .
Lifted dripping from the past, it's summer 1935,
coffee on the terrace overlooking the crowds
and pigeons of the Plaza Mayor. Relatives,
near and distant, coming to call and appraise.
Afternoons she'd sit at the piano, practicing
Granados. The sense of gathering clouds. . . .
She had met Luís in Genoa ten months earlier,
where his export business took him twice yearly.
Her Grand Tour—rather laxly chaperoned
by a stylish widowed cousin. Mathilda's mixture
of Miss Porter polish and New York impertinence
had turned his head. Nor, for that matter, did she
lack masses of marcelled blond curls. A month's time
and they'd overcome objections from both sets
of parents. No one was going to be impoverished,
on the contrary, and Mathilda already knew enough

Spanish not to be cowed by Luís's grandmother,
whom they visited at La Glorieta, half a day
north of Madrid. Hot afternoons there, young
women in white aprons brought sherbets with mint
and set them down with either a yawn or a smile
as you gossiped under the vine-shadowed pergola.
It all might have gone on forever, but then came
the war, the hateful, unjust, cruel war, Oh, Luís. . . .

She gets up and goes to the photograph
of Margareta and the grandchildren, taken
five Christmases ago in Lisbon. But it's not
the day to dawdle, she has to take large-print
books to Papa, some papers to sign, a hot pad,
and his medication. Visiting hours at the home
are rather strict. A glance out the window
to the back garden. Oh, there's Ernesto already—
getting the roses wet, as he's been told not to.
Honestly, what does it take with some people?
And eighty invited will be milling about
on the lawn tomorrow for the theater benefit.
How we ever let ourselves be persuaded—.
Her eye lights on an old painted fan framed
and hanging next to the writing desk, a brooding
majo paying court to his eternal beloved
of the moment, mantilla and pink satin slippers—
Luís's first present. *Pedazo de mi alma,*
she quotes him, bites her lip, and leaves the room.)

8.

1974

I'm with Walter now, he's driving, we've left
D.C. behind as we make our way northwest
through Maryland to Harper's Ferry—our first
road trip together, one of the scarce occasions
when we have time to go into our origins.
In shards and fragments, he gives the story
of his ancestors, gentlemen farmers in Hungary,
the War, the betrayals, the grandfather who
didn't survive Auschwitz;
the grandmother who did, her life as a cook
in Catskill resort hotels, lately retired
at a group home in Detroit. His own mother's death.
Silence and a hand placed lightly on his
are as much as I can do. Trees rushing by,
a sinking sun caught in them. Wordlessness,
more than anything else, was how we communicated.

Five o'clock when we arrive, but there's time
to stand on a bluff overlooking the handsome
confluence of the Potomac and Shenandoah,
several houses from the early 1800s
quietly regarding us while a twilight
soft as down creeps in from all sides,
scent of chestnut leaf and flower expanding,
a distant plash of waters, and the whispered
sensation of backward-stretching time, remote
and deep as Appalachia. A brief promenade's
muffled footfalls resound with the gravity
lent to any earth where blood was once shed.

On to Virginia, a hotel booked within sight
of the Blue Ridge. After dinner in our top-floor room
a windowseat offers the best prospect of the moon

levitating over black foothills, night breezes
heavy with perfume from flowers on the silk tree
below—a favorite species of Mr. Jefferson's,
I recall reading somewhere. From the pint flask
that used to go everywhere with me I've poured
a double shot these ice cubes will only halfway
cool down. Out over the lawn, fireflies bestir
themselves, rise, signal. An image floats up,
how five summers ago Ann and I caught them and turned
Mason jars into short-term, green-flickering lamps.
Would she remember that? I'll ask when we meet
next month. But wait, what was—? A bright strobe
wide as the sky switches on, sheet-lightning playing
back and forth to the roll of monumental drums, and then
bang, another crackling flashbulb, the air charged
with electric prickles. Walter comes over, lounges
next to me and shares the light show. When
I turn, there's that serious-edged smile of his,
solemn eyes that seem to see everything. To break
the silence I ask, "Ever hear that old song, *Oh,
Shenandoah?*" I sing a few notes, a few wordless notes.

A few more, as we veered among the shifting vistas
of Skyline Drive in bright morning sunlight,
Milky Ways of wild daisies waving from roadside,
white and gold dots against windblown grasses.
Most worries seemed trivial up there on the blue
rooftop of Virginia, the "mother of presidents."
Conversation turned to poetry, that year's
paramount topic since things I'd written were now
appearing in print, the hoped-for endorsement
at last conferred. I didn't grasp how rare
his *a priori* support of the fantastic
project was, while I soldiered on without much

worrying about income, seconded by him,
an architect in the line of Wright and Kahn.
When we came down from the Blue Ridge, it was only
to push on to Charlottesville, the university
and another celebrated hill outside town, site
of our most versatile president's house.
The estate implied to some of its visitors
that those ideal, white-elephant fantasies
Americans have always had a weakness for at times
come true as shrine of beauty or cradle of thought
that then sets forth to revise the status quo.
Guided change, I mean, since nothing,
in any case, ever stays the same. Even us.
We had two more years until dividing forces
clearer to me now than they were then sent him
elsewhere. But a quality of wordlessness
is still within reach, present in the snapshot
before me right now, and still emitting energy.
Hands on hips he smiles, standing beneath
frozen hands of the clock set over the door
of the domed house that has become the house we share.

(Henry Barstow in a field outside Front Royal
watches his son Billy tote the .22 he gave him
for his birthday. Safety's on, but the boy isn't
easy with it, clearly. He's just ten, an only child.
Henry's own twelve-gauge is like an extra trusty limb.
A little target practice and the boy'll feel handier
with his rifle. Morning sunlight flickering with wind
in the distant hickories. Billy stops and stoops down
to see something. "Look, Daddy, a butterfly."
Swallowtail flits up in the light, the boy smiles
at him. "It was drinking this pink flower." Nods
and says, "Let's keep moving, we've got a ways to go."
Yes, there's no better land anywhere. Henry plans

to turn over the farm to his boy one day, but maybe
Billy ought not to farm, no money in it. Hateful
what the world's become, lot of crooks running things.
If he sells up they'll just turn his farm into
a development. But what if he was forced to? Why,
Granddaddy'd climb out of his grave and knock him
cockeyed. Six generations on this farm. Well,
he probably won't have to. A redtail hawk floats
overhead. There. A likely stump to shoot at—
but where's Billy? Oh. Running up and holding out
a little bunch of wildflowers. "Here, Daddy, I picked
these for you." Billy's face changes when he stares
at him. "We don't have time for those, Son." Boy bites
his lip, looks down at the flowers. Henry has to choke
back the temptation to get mad, knows he shouldn't,
but, God, he doesn't want his son to turn out like that.
Life is hard enough and he cares for this boy more
than he knows how to say. "Here, Son, let's get some
practice with your gun." Bends down and takes it,
squats behind the boy. "Hold it like this." Stiffly.
"See that stump?" No answer. Then Billy turns around:
"Daddy? I'm scared." Their eyes lock. Who is more afraid?
In deep distance, a short blast from a train whistle,
the rush of eastbound wheels on steel, a gleam of light
across the miles; and the gritty taste of disappointment.)

9.

1989

Misgivings this December dusk are one mood
with falling snow that wipers left to right and back
brush off the windshield in crystal wedges,
things coming clear, then going dim again as I
try for some perspective. After the breakup
I'd planned at least two years of singlehood,
but here I am, caught off guard, launching out again,
even though we're both still in shock, even
though we live in different states, and my stint
in Cincinnati over with. Along the highway,
near a turnoff to Chillicothe, an old farm
swims into view, barn and house and one bare elm
reading as an oblique lithograph, endurance
in fine degrees of white and gray and solitude.
(Odd how that attic window's the only one lighted.)
When and where will I see you again? We'll write,
of course, a cool replacement for the kiss
still tingling on my ear, oh, *not* the last—.
The two hours to Columbus don't seem daunting
yet, and once there I can decide to stop
or go on. . . . (It turns out simple persistence and
the steady metronomic clearance of the windshield
suffice to get my blue Colt far as Akron
before it turns into a lit-up Holiday Inn.)

By morning strong sun is out and snow melting.
Today's offbeat itinerary: a wary drive
through Kent State to see where law and order
was once, no matter how, enforced; and Hiram College,
alma mater of a friend who'd been a life-raft
during the stormy year just past. Small town
Midwestern virtues are what I see in Hiram's
red brick, foursquare layout, its blending in

with the houses of the citizens—a public
peace and reliability that to New Yorkers
can only seem exotic as . . . as a cornfield. From there
to Garrettsville, Hart Crane's birthplace nine decades
earlier, though no bronze plaque anywhere tells
which weathered old gingerbread Gothic fantasy
belonged to Mr. Crane and his young bride. That one,
I arbitrarily decide and pay respects,
before continuing on to I-80 at Youngstown.
Hour by hour in the back of my mind you hover,
up and down over the Alleghenies, a glaze
of light on stands of evergreen, or the hush
that holds motionless flotillas of cloud high
above in a blue that seems to promise everything
without precisely spelling out what everything might be.

(Walker Tuggs steps down stiffly into the sunlight,
the door of the trailer slowly drifting shut.
He locks it. His trick knee hurts but he has to get
some groceries in. Drives to the Oak Mall.
A new check-out girl stares a bit, he being
one of the few colored in Columbiana County.
Nobody 72 with eyes can be surprised at that,
and by now it sure doesn't trouble him. Stare
right back. He's from Cincinnati, his people
go back to Kentucky and the underground railroad
but he prefers northern Ohio. Daughter still down there,
takes tickets at the Harriet Beecher Stowe House,
not ever going to marry. She keeps his paintings
in her back parlor, not a scrap of extra room here.
Years since anybody lifted a hand to sell them.
He unloads the Voyager, takes the stuff inside.
Not too many trailers installed in this park
and it's next to a nice stretch of woodland.
He might get back to painting some time.

Why, since he's been totally forgotten?
Well now. It could have gone different. He puts
the cans of Heinz beans on the shelf, the ribs
and six-pack in the fridge. In the late '30s,
they grouped him with protest painting just because
his subject was "the soul of black folk."
A few critics took interest, and then collectors.
Somewhere in the Museum of Modern Art's storage,
an early Walker Tuggs is a-moldering in its grave. . . .
After the war, he went back to work and *better* work,
but the scene had changed. And so had Harlem.
Things weren't so friendly, besides, deep down,
what we had was an Ohio boy, strictly cornbread
and collard greens, champagne didn't do that much
for him, and abstraction, why, next to nothing.
Abstract is just the skeleton you start with,
you got to put meat on the bones. Sure, he did
a couple of shows, but they didn't rock the rafters.
And he wasted a lot of time on a no-good broad,
and a lot of money at the races, ain't blaming
nobody. Seems like he always had a way of saying
the wrong thing, arrogant s.o.b. that he was.
And because he attended a few Party meetings,
word went out "Tuggs is a Commie," which was a lie,
he'd just gone to hear Paul Robeson speak.
Oh yes, a lot of people let him know one way
or another they were on his side, but handshakes
behind the scenes don't pay the rent, do they?
Most folks don't have a notion about what's good
anyhow till somebody with guts says real loud
which horse to pick, and then they trample each
other trying to bet on it. A gas, except if
you're not the favorite. Finally he got fed up,
came back to Cincy, drove a truck for P & G,
painted houses, married, lived in Over-the-Rhine,

and sometimes, of a Sunday afternoon, set up the easel.
Little Marlene would run up and grab his pants leg
and bother him, or Bertis would say fix the broken
lamp, so he didn't finish, why, three canvases a year.
Mr. Tyrone, his old teacher, died, about the last person
who was interested anyhow, and one day, blam, he
pitched the oil paints into the trash and went
on a three-day tear. Hasn't painted a lick since.
After Bertis died, he moved up to Youngstown,
lived with a gal who worked in a beauty salon
and sang weekends at the Flying Eagle Tavern.
He remembers one time Dakota Staton dropped by,
eventually gave in and did a song with the band.
Nice lady. Wasn't too long after that Jonelle
got on dope and in a month or two was good
for nothing, so he eased on out. He'll still go
into Youngstown now and then, whenever, you know,
the mood strikes to hear a little jazz music.
Columbiana has its share of two-bit rednecks,
but mostly they don't bother you if you don't them.
He sits down on the bed, reaches for the racing form,
by accident pushing *The Vindicator*
and a book of Romare Bearden's art to the floor.
Picks it up and looks at a few pictures,
goes back to the magazine. *Damn,* left the tap
dripping. Groans as he gets up, damn arthritis
in his knee. Sound of a car outside. Hold it,
what's that? Somebody knocking. He goes
first to the window. White fellow, sport jacket,
no tie, carrying a briefcase. Opens: "Yes?"
"Mr. Walker Tuggs?" "What do you want?"
Guy smiles. "The painter, Walker Tuggs?"
"I am. What can I do for you." Smiles again:
"Whew, did I have trouble finding you. May I come in?")

10

1977

An early fall swept in, the yellow leaf
flecked tobacco brown by late September
when we drove up to Boston to attend
the funeral. Only in his last year
had we met him, but not everyone is
Robert Lowell and the impression made
had been rapid, sharp, hypnotic. A friend
wrote out directions how to find the Church
of the Advent among brickfront houses
at the foot of Beacon Hill. His mourners
were already assembled when we got there,
among them, faces known from book jackets.
(A pew ahead sat Saul Bellow, who nodded
as friends passed.) Finally the first widow
strode alone and hatless down the aisle
to the front. The second, in a wide straw,
and flanked by daughters, looked left and right
with a tentative English stare. A number
of those present were, to judge by a familiar
set of features, Lowell cousins. Prayers
and scripture. His oldest writer friend
Peter Taylor read "Where the Rainbow Ends."
Dark woodwork of the Neo-Gothic interior
gleamed in half light. The organ poured
out old sherries by Bach and Stainer,
the liturgy unenthusiastic, as befit
a standing now reverting to the deceased.
I thought back to the times we'd met,
of strenuous opinions cobbled together so
we wouldn't be marooned on the barrenness
of monologue, and to merit his attention—
which how many are ever willing to grant,
even to the recommended young? No further

chance to earn it. Afterwards, outside,
cheerful words and a smile from Dick W.,
an intelligent handshake from Robert P.
Car doors opened for the striking daughter,
for the little English son. A William Morris
pattern of oak leaves on the pavement, bare
black branches above, the silver Boston light,
traffic noise from over toward the Common.
With so little circumstance, a chapter ends.

(To be Martha Diodati is to peep from a dormer
window down onto Chestnut Street, gaze fixed
on a solitary pedestrian moving like a stylus
along the pavement. She wouldn't know him,
oh, but she might have once. Things rust,
they frazzle: people didn't always drive
everywhere. It's fearful, "even at my age,
dear, even then." Speaking in that rippling
way Mother had, like braille, feel it,
but you don't want to, naturally, unless
you've got a thing for insects. Spiders, too.
Brrr, there was one yesterday. Not as many
as had been at the Institute, thank God
that's been whirled away on the wings of the storm.
WE SOMETIMES MAKE MISTAKES. Have and will.
Although. It could be less sad here, less sour,
with one cushion for the past, another for rumor.
Didn't *use* to lie. Conscience makes you, because
you can't stroke their fur the wrong way. Can't.
The only reason not to have gone ahead
with the marriage is, we knew it wouldn't
do, ever, not in a million years. All right,
if there's medicine to be swallowed, so be it.
Just because a person is cowardly in one
direction doesn't mean she is in another.

No, that wasn't our point. Wait. Lost the thread.
Why don't you listen? DON'T WANT TO. Abuse
of power. Now, this drawer wasn't locked before.
DON'T PRETEND the playing cards AREN'T IN it.
The idea that silver spoons are hiding there, too,
is just an excuse. Clarinda's present of a yellow
silk purse, oh dear, how many eons ago,
with but *one spoon* in it, for medicine,
otherwise, none. No more. Miss her awfully.
She doesn't come now. Said she was housebound,
like everybody else. But you lose track, eh?
Beans for lunch today and so it's Saturday,
but, otherwise, who would know? They'll never
tell, that much is certain. Abandoned to one's
relatives, a well-known disaster. But then,
there's nowhere else, not the Institute, never.
And there's the trust to manage, just can't.
Get tied in knots, the Gordian knot, it
won't let go, let you alone. Stop it, stop
it right now. OH, a slap. Please help. Stop.
Stop it up. So there. You were warned. They said.
It can be borne. But so sad. Why people bother.
Granted, there's nothing hateful about stretching
out on the sofa. If only one weren't alone.
When we were little, we took afternoon naps,
but there's no point in that now. Hmm.
Uncle Abner brought pictures of dinosaurs—
the one with all the teeth, so terrifying.
He tried to be comforting, but it seemed . . .
wrong, very wrong. That very sofa, heavens,
keep forgetting, and then remembering. Well,
he's gone. Never tattled. We don't do that.
It would be. Like. Smashing the. Window to bits.)

11.

1985

It was eccentric to leave one vacation spot
for another, but under the muggy August
stillness of eastern Vermont, one of us began
to mutter, the other to sigh about ocean air—
after all, within driving distance, right? Last week
of the month we set out through New Hampshire
all the way to Portsmouth and up I-95
to Maine. Among tidepools at Ogunquit
a seagull choked down a starfish, as textured
breezes scented with seaweed and beach roses
buffeted our sunburned faces, while out beyond
the whitecaps one sail sharp as a palette-knife
cut into the wind. A hike along the "Marginal
Way" was led unawares by a blond teenager
in Hawaiian shorts, tanned back gleaming with sweat
ten strides ahead of us, his taunts to friends
farther on a thought-free epitome of what
it meant to be eighteen.
                        Well, on to Kennebunk,
where at least one guest house had rooms, the owner
a source of hush-hush directions out to Walker Point,
for discreet spying on our VP's establishment.
Nothing extraordinary, except its site—and ranks
of formidable palisades patrolled by guards
barking into walkie-talkies. (He'd postponed
his normal summer leave till August in order
to stand by during Reagan's cancer surgery;
but wasn't in evidence anywhere that day.)

Next morning to Portland. An hour spent
scouting out the woodframe birthplace
of the author whose fable of Evangeline
Bellefontaine and Gabriel Lajeunesse

sticks in the mind more than any given verses.
The old town had already vanished by the time
he lamented "My Lost Youth," hardly the last
casualty of modernism. But a relic sense
of the early republic smilingly adhered
to his house—in the fading, primitive florets
of the wallpaper, translucent curtains damp
with sea air, the tick of an antique clock. . . .

Our goal: the shabby-genteel resort of Newagen,
low rock ledges out front suitable lookouts
for a sun also in decline but unapologetic
about its extravagant setting, as with hindered
dignity it descended like a blind and blinding
old visionary among continents of golden cloud
that slowly cooled and reassembled wine-stained
ramparts over the last red lavas in the west.
Always the dreamlike breathing of bay waters,
stirred by long smooth swells that took their hue
from the larger dream the heavens had become.

Mid-November a divorcée from Teaneck would
snap up our Vermont retreat, which despite
amenities previous antiquarian owners
had lent it—mammoth fireplace in working order,
stencilled walls, a garden filled with lilies
and plots of bergamot the hangout of darting
ruby-throats—had to be let go. Too far
from the "primary residence," subject to theft,
vandalism, and leaks, the Colonial fixtures
kept up to snuff at ridiculous cost.
"The art of losing isn't hard to master."
Yesterday, rummaging in the back of a high shelf,
my hand lighted on a jar of sweet-and-sour relish
put up from the bumper crop of cucumbers

our kitchen garden produced that summer.
I read the label and the date, hand-written
in purple ink; and all of this came back.

(Gene Gerard had forgotten it was his birthday,
but on the other hand, who cares, if you're doing
time at Grafton County Correctional Facility?
He didn't tell anybody because he'd still have
to slop the hogs and all the rest of it. Spent
an extra half hour in the weight room, and then
there was a card and letter from his sister Marie,
but it didn't say much, which figures, since nothing
much ever happens in Lewiston. He didn't expect
anything from Marilynne, since she hasn't written
once since he got here. OK, so it's his fault
getting drunk and saying the things he did
that last night. He'd gotten annoyed because,
after the argument before, she'd put a sign
out on the lawn saying NIGHTCRAWLERS 2 CENTS.
And he knew she wasn't really planning to go
out behind the house and dig fishing worms
at two pennies a head. He said so in language
he shouldn't have used. Nor was it very smart
to duke it out with the cop that slapped
a D.U.I. on him. But if you've put away
better than a fifth of Seagram's and are
el fucko to the gills, these are risks you run.

He doesn't remember all that much about how
he drove down here. He'd gone to the Deck,
probably the raunchiest bar in Lewiston,
then phoned a buddy of his in New Hampshire
and said, get ready, he was coming. Rick, see,
goes back to Army days, but since he opened
a used-car dealership outside of Lebanon,

he's settled down some. The greatest time
they had together was right after discharge
when they decided to attend the *Soldier of Fortune*
convention in Las Vegas. Drunk the whole time,
and he's not real sure what the programs were,
but does remember a blonde from Columbia,
South Carolina, named Nickie. She sweet-talked
them into driving her back home, there were
friends they could stay with and so forth.
Got only as far as New Orleans, though,
where she checked out on them, no explanation
why. Never forget that bar in Oklahoma City
when she got up on stage and lip-synched
a Reba McEntire song, wearing jeans and a bra.

Anyway, coming back home to stack two-by-fours
at Ace Lumber and Roofing wasn't exactly
the most fun idea he could think of, but
just what was he supposed to do? He couldn't
get in college if he tried, the only thing
he ever did well in his life was drink and play
shortstop, but we're not talking about pro
ball here. Like, suppose you're deep down bored
with your life, then what? He asked Marilynne
that question once. She told him he was cracked,
which he knew, and which MasterCard also knew
when they stopped credit. He only owes five
thousand bucks—in other words, no way in Hell
to pay it back. Especially from jail. Earlier
that afternoon after chores, when he was coming in,
he saw one of the old people on the porch
of the rest home next door—that's what happens
in New Hampshire if you're aged and can't
support yourself: they put you next to the prison
and maybe eventually a relative will take pity

and pull you out. Anyhow, this old guy
waved and it reminded him of when Granddad
was alive. He kept in shape, so they'd throw
to each other for an hour or two, and Granddad
would tell him about his old man who was half
Abenaki Indian and half French Canadian,
a logger up near Bethel. And once Granddad saw
Roosevelt when he stopped in Augusta on his way
to Campobello Island, during the war. Shortly
after, he was called up. Shipped him to Guam.
Had a heart attack five years ago, then
Grandma died of a stroke six months later.
The old house they had was sold, knocked down,
and an Exxon built on the lot. Mama got some
of the proceeds but hasn't mentioned sharing.

He lies down on the bunk and opens the card
again, a cartoon of Garfield the Cat scarfing
down a piece of birthday cake, with the message
"Sweet thoughts for my wildcat of a brother
on his birthday." He hears a portable radio
playing and smells something sharp. Oh, blowing
weed again, the next cell over, like always.
Easier to get drugs in this place than outside.
That was Nickie's thing, she liked coke. And vodka.
And your charge card. And getting what she wanted.)

12.

1978

Coolness of late April in Berkeley,
actually, Kensington, where I'll stay
two nights and give a reading down at the U.
Prescription sunglasses are fending off
steam-white morning sun in Simon's garden as I
revise a poem begun last month after a visit
to Wallace Stevens' grave near Hartford.
From branches of fruit trees nearby come
intricate pipings and wing-flutter, the air
laced with scents of hard-to-place flowers,
of eucalyptus and the medicinal taint
of malathion drifting over from next door.
A framework of ideas down on the page—but now
the instinct to protect and feed them wakes up.
What exactly do we do when we revise?
Hopes of enjoying more than what's there move
across unrhythmed first thoughts to sound out
the play of word against word, psychic antennae
alert for enharmonic changes clearing vistas
onto a penetration that we hadn't known
or felt how much we meant, until the right note
sends thrums of voltage up the spine (a home
remedy for professional infirmities
like scoliosis writers tend to have)
or like the smart crack of bat against ball,
along with heightened tone in mind and muscle—
the product of recreation (also, of work)
as if we played a sport whose goal was truth.

At noon, Simon drives me across Bay Bridge,
nodding toward volunteer wood sculptures out
on the mud flats, including one that people call
the "Trojan Rabbit." In fact, a kind of epic aura
wreathes the approaching skyline, symphonic masses

of cloud and fog obscuring the topless towers. . . .
But sunlit, open-air cafes ambling past
as we thread our way through up- and downhill
streets are plain as day, with not a single
omen of disaster, human losses that
begin to surface three short years from now.

We're having lunch on Polk Street with the editor
of *Gay Sunshine.* Cracked crab with lobster sauce,
herbed green beans, sourdough bread and a dry
Napa Valley wine remind me that California's
the only place outside France where pleasure
is taken seriously. On that topic, we'll go
some hours later for jasmine tea with Edouard R.,
temporarily settled near Golden Gate Park,
but, as the constant flow of anecdote suggests,
a permanent citizen of cosmopolis.
Last summer in Belgrade. Paris in 1931.
Khartoum, Tangier, Capri, Chania.
Pound, Breton, Toklas. . . . Did we need further proof
that authors' lives were once less drab, less
homebound than ours today? No, but factor in
the case of Stevens, who, though seldom stirring
from his Hartford attic, still explored
interior searoads and gulfs farther out
and deeper than his situation seemed to promise—
"The old age of a watery realist"—
unless that other grave ecstatic got it right
when she said: "There is no frigate like a book."

(Chuck Yuen, 21, strolls across Portsmouth Square,
doesn't stop to join the crowd gathered to watch
a kung-fu expert smashing and kicking thin air
as though fighting for his life. He remembers how
the hoods on Jackson Street used to want him to pick

a gang and he wouldn't. They beat him up once but
after that left him alone. He looks at the old guys
playing checkers, squinting through their glasses
at the board, without talking. At a distance
the Transamerica pyramid hooks a passing cloud
on its point, then lets it go. Confused feelings.
He went with a white guy to the guy's place on Powell
last night and stayed until after one. Mother
didn't say anything this morning—it's Sunday—
but she looked at him hard. Just to break
the silence he asked was she feeling better,
and she said yes. She's being treated for TB,
a light case, but still. She sat down by a lamp
underneath that old picture of a boat in a storm,
a Chinese-style of a boat with pointed sails,
and began to sew on a button. She looked old. Father'd
already gone to play cards with a friend over
in the Richmond, but he never asks questions anyway.
Besides, this isn't a problem you could take
to the Six Companies, which is about all Father
knows except for working as a mail carrier.
He's OK, but they don't talk about stuff. A cold
wave of fear comes over him: If people heard.
Chuck has known what he wanted to do for a while,
but not where to do it, or who with, or how. This guy
just had the guts to come up and start talking.
And the rest was automatic. Also, kind of heavy.
Which doesn't mean that next week everything
won't get back to normal. He'll show up at his job
at the record store, he'll watch people go by
on the street—and maybe one of them will be
this guy, who gave him his number and said call.
For some reason he thinks back to grade school,
when a few of the kids would spit at the new ones
from Hong Kong and say they weren't Americans.

He never wanted to do that, even if his family
had been here four generations. It wasn't fair,
besides, they were already scared from not knowing
English. Some of them went into gangs later on.
His mother always made him come when school let out
to the garment sweatshop where she worked, at least,
until he was almost nine. She told him not
to go wandering around in the streets. Like now.
He sees another guy, Chinese though, staring at him.
And thinks: Maybe it's obvious to people. Is that bad
or good? Am I that way, really? It's like asking
am I Asian or American. . . . He passes a line
of old guys reading the newspaper in the window
of *The Chinese Times* and remembers how
his grandfather, who was a typesetter, used to say,
"I'm American. I've never left the United States
and probably won't ever go. But China is inside me."
Chuck met a monk last week who'd been to Singapore,
not a Catholic monk, some other denomination,
forgot what he said. These monks have a house
over in the Mission District, sometimes wear robes
and sometimes not. This one had been a brother
for twenty years, had gray hair and a kind look.
A guy skating on the sidewalk had knocked
into him and he fell. Chuck helped him up, so
they got to talking. Eventually he explained
he was Catholic but didn't get to church much.
The brother didn't tell him that was a sin,
which was a relief, but did say come to the house
any time and have dinner with them. Maybe he'll go
one of these days. He walks past a restaurant named
The Golden Mountain, sees his reflection in the glass
against characters painted in gold, most of which
he can't read—but maybe are inside him anyway, like
Grandfather said, even though he's never been to China.)

13.

1989

Last week of the year and there's a pall
of cloud over East Texas, roughly the same
color as the parched stretch of desert
dotted with sage the interstate divides,
a bone-white ribbon receding steadily west.
Thoughts come back from the trek through
nearly two years ago, when Sandy and I turned
onto state 71 just past Columbus, to make
a detour to Austin. The same cloud cover
that day also. Ladybird Johnson's policy
of public "beautification" had taken the form
of sowing wildflowers in colorful masses
along the highway shoulders—native lupine,
poppy, and daisies, mile after speeding mile.
Suddenly a flashing light: rats, the state patrol.
Forgot we'd left behind laissez-faire I-10.
It was pointless to argue. Ticket accepted,
we drove on to see our friends in Austin,
who sympathized with stories of their own
and took us to limestone cliffs above the river
for views of the old capital, identified
at dusk when a lone star rose and branded
the blue evening with its silver light.

That was then. This time I've taken I-20
to have a look at Dallas and Fort Worth (among
other attractions, the Kimbell Museum,
Louis Kahn's not yet surpassed temple of art).
A low-level disquiet buzzes through daydreams
as Nashville artists on the radio keep advising,
"All you need in life is one good well,"
or, "Love helps those who cannot help themselves."
And then the engine slings a rod and ratchets
nastily to a halt in the middle of nowhere.

Don't ever try to flag down cars with cruise
control set at 80 along straightaways in Texas.
Deep gratitude to Leroy Byrom of Des Moines
for giving me a lift into Dallas. He'd been
to see his folks in Little Rock and, as we drove,
played gospel songs composed and sung by him
an Albuquerque entrepreneur had promised
to do something with. His creamed-coffee hand
shook mine goodbye when he dropped me off
at a Howard Johnson's near the first exit
to Dallas. "Have a good life," I was urged
and have actually attempted to manage,
the first step a telephone call to triple-A,
who sent rescue in the form of a Ford tow truck.

(Victor Lopez of Arlington takes down
the genealogy he's been working on several years,
ever since he decided to find out about his roots.
The first part was easy, given his family
had records of the original grant on the Brazos
River, in what was called the Nile Valley
because of floods that struck from time to time
and redesigned the basin. Weren't many Jews
in Texas then, they didn't have a rabbi,
but observed as best they could. Before that
there were Lopez in Mexico and had been
since around 1650, emigrants from Brazil.
They'd come to Rio from southern France,
where the family had been living since Spain
kicked out everyone who wasn't Catholic.
First mention is of Arie ben Jacob of Toledo,
a metalsmith, whose son went to Avignon
after the expulsion and used the name Louppes.

The sound of a firetruck outside blares, subsides.
Victor makes some notes about other branches

of the family and then the telephone rings.
His wife Sharon, her voice tentative, whispery.
Nothing in particular, just wanted to talk.
"Look, I was thinking maybe a visit with Mother
tonight, OK? Want to come?" He agrees, hangs up.
She hasn't been well. At first they looked into
Epstein-Barr virus but finally decided
it was just depression. Began with her losing
her job at Houston and Klein Attorneys. People
being laid off because of the sluggish economy.
His gallery of Mexican antiques was doing poorly,
too, so no funds this year for private school,
which upset her because it was like starting out
with a handicap, and she hated that for the kids.
He promised to tutor them; but admitted the problem
was more complex. What can you do? But this will end,
and there's enough to see them through, just have
to wait it out. He had started going to Torah
study after temple on Saturdays, but Sharon wouldn't,
said that wasn't her family tradition. Victor
wishes she had something to get her out of herself.
He can't do much. The doctor's going to try Elavil.
Hope it's the right thing. Sam and Becky have been
kind of clingy lately, as though they'd regressed
a few years. He has to talk to them a lot,
what with Sharon staying in her room so they
won't see her crying. He thinks briefly of his
father's death, the kaddish, and sitting shiva.
Death is the only thing you don't have a chance
for a comeback. One day you're not. It's like a plank
that the person ahead of you walks—him first,
then it's your turn. Meanwhile you have your work,
and your family, things you care about. A few words
from kaddish float into his mind. The gold letters
on the spines of the books over his desk
glow in the afternoon light. *Blessed be He. . . .*

80

Been thinking of a ski trip to Steamboat Springs,
the kids, too, they say they want to learn. Sometimes
it's better to *pretend* things are going great,
then, like magic, they are. It's for Sharon.
A change of scene, a change of luck. The Rockies—
fantastic. Aspen's where they had their honeymoon.)

14

1990

Palm trees along Santa Monica Boulevard,
puffs of domed cloud over the sea
and sleek Art Deco buildings
in the chalk-white light of March
set me adrift in a self-directed road movie
as I glided and wove among (Côte d'Azur
of the mind) the pastel sports cars, then turned
into a parking lot beside the theater.
A recently released *Henry V*—
the same director-actor whose *Midsummer
Night's Dream* was playing at the Taper Forum—
was what I'd come up with as a way
to fend off anxiously replayed projections
of your arrival here tomorrow. Would we
still feel as we did three months ago?
Be calm, enjoy the film. (Its freshest scene,
the young king's courtship of his lady—broken
music of her modest franglais and his
regal, boyish "maker of manners" dismissal
of French constraint in favor of a kiss.)

WELCOME TO LOS ANGELES says the sign, and here
by the freeway the red-lettered name of the concrete
construction company repairing embrasures
on an overpass is CAST OF THOUSANDS. The smile
that breaks across your bearded face when I point
toward it's worth these anxious weeks of waiting.
A cast of thousands's what in fact we have,
thousands of thousands here in this sneak preview
21st century on the Pacific Rim.
The Carnation sign looming over La Brea
if divided into two words sums it up

as the headless, tailless millipede
of cars, vans, and trucks creeps up 405
or down El Camino Real, my blue Colt
a single frame in a round-the-clock feature
that unpredictably jams but then resumes,
in a rhythm accepted by the stoic habitué,
each at last carried miraculously home.
A cast of thousands—but in this little
sublet house near the canals of Venice,
with palms, and poinsettias bright red even
now in the vigilant porch light, we are
only two, the door closed on everything
but the music, the candle, a dozen
carnations bought on last-minute impulse
that afternoon along with a sack of navel oranges
from a Chicano kid who, hesitant, trustful,
made the exchange from a traffic island on Fairfax.
Local wisdom says once you've merged top speed
onto I-10, rocketing west into the red ball
of six o'clock sun, "There's no turning back now."
One by one, defenses fall away, not strong enough
to cap the burning well, intensities I had
forgotten or no longer felt entitled to.

And when, two weeks later, we say goodbye,
What then? "If it's meant to continue, we'll
find a way." We will. Differences between us
are, possibly, what is most promising. A year's
wait, or more, we can manage if required to.
The royal palms stir and gesture agreement;
cloud terraces poise over the sea and put down
Feelers of light on molten waves where closer in
silhouettes of surfers crouch and zigzag forward
as a jet overhead wheels into its eastbound track.

(Kimberley Sternberg closes the door behind her
softly since Kevin has fallen asleep at last.
She left a note: "Dear Mr. Shanahan, Sleep well.
Your secret admirer returns tomorrow. Be ready."
The jeep backs out onto Spaulding, drops into first.
A deep breath. Feels great to have a night out.
Since Kevin was diagnosed a year ago, it's been
rocky. A lot of hours every day go to help out—
but if you're not there for your best friend,
what are you? "I hate AIDS," she sighs and sets
her jaw, lets herself wonder how long he's got and
how long before she has to find a new roommate.
Receptionists aren't paid all that well,
and rent in West Hollywood just keeps inflating.
Kevin gave up his work doing continuity for
Warner, just stays home and watches soaps all day.
He decided against any more injections for the lesions,
just too painful, don't let anybody tell you
interferon feels good when it goes under your skin.
He'd planned to go to Maui for a few days, then the guy
who'd invited him canceled for no real reason.
Kevin's been pleading with her for weeks to go out
and have fun, so when Todd telephoned from Sedona,
she said, sure, they could meet, love to. You have
to be flexible with Todd, he's always on location,
you never know when he'll call. In love with him?
Yes. No. Since there's no real possibility.
She's getting tired, though, of hearing Tanya's
soundbites about what a mistake getting involved
with married guys is. People do what they have to do.
Wouldn't you know the nail on her middle finger'd
break this morning when she was trying to unscrew
the lid of a jar of buckwheat honey. Oh well.

She turns onto Sunset, and wonders why Todd always
has to stay at the Beverly Hills, invariably

in one of the bungalows out back. Advantage is,
she knows the drill: you park in that little street
behind the hotel, follow a path between palm trees
and shrubbery right up to the swimming pool
and the bungalows. That way you skip the front desk
so nobody has to know that Todd's seeing someone
and maybe tell Renée, not to mention the tabloids.
How *do* those guys put up with being trailed
by flashbulbs everywhere they go? Oh, a full moon,
how mushy. She remembers the last time she was here
a hooker was doing exactly the same thing—like, what
else could the girl have been, in that leather getup?—
and they kind of smiled at each other, which made
her feel weird. Yes, but when Todd opened the door,
she stepped into his arms and pretended to be that girl . . .
and so when they came up for air, Todd said, "Hey,
that wasn't a kiss, that was a breathalyzer."
And on from there. She looks in the rearview mirror,
turns her head from side to side, puts on more lipstick
and blots it, the duller red imprint on the Kleenex
symmetrical, parted, split with white. Wads it up,
steps out, locks the car, and then sees the silhouette
of a big guy standing there staring at her, not moving.
Oh, a cop. "See your driver's licence, please?")

15.

Coming back at the end of our last Northwest summer,
Ann and I decided to take the ferry across
Lake Michigan. A night in Escanaba,
which turned out to be something of a resort.
We noticed a weathered beauty queen—blonde,
wearing a white suit and seagreen blouse,
Chanel bag swinging from long gold chain—
walk unsteadily into the Escanaba Hotel
with her partner (in a dark blazer, also tipsy).
Cocktail piano tinkled "Stardust" and "As Time
Goes By" through the foyer, a stylishly
maritime atmosphere from the lake underscored
by bits of netting on the walls, shells, wheels,
cork floats. After dinner, up in our room, an hour
or two to sort through snapshots from the last
few months, who would keep which, and why. Somber
courtesy had governed every word and deed
all summer. Was it imaginative concern
anticipating the moment when we'd send
each other separate ways with a wan smile
and parental pat on the shoulder? Meanwhile
here were the pictures, what, of sky-blue gentians
and scarlet monkeyflowers in a grassy meadow
near Logan Pass high up in Glacier Park.
Or trembling aspens by a run of white water.
Or the Pacific, seen from Mount Neahkahnie.
Oh, somehow to keep what has been lived, this
perishable choreography of our pathfinding
through the years. . . . I paused over a shot
of the South Dakota Badlands, burnt lunar rocks
where nothing grew, the only sound a hidden chitter
of desert crickets. Now, even two months after,
shimmering heatwaves boiled up and scorched my hand.

Next day, our car in the hold, we stood on deck
to watch the churning wake dissipate farther
and farther behind into the orange track of the sun.
A blast from the stack seemed to echo that other
steamship passage a short four years ago
when we'd boarded a liner bound for France.
A briefer trek, this one, not a crossing
to the Old World. It was, in fact, the home
stretch, endowed with whatever advantages
accrue to realism, so that without forcing
I could see intelligence and experience
at my side, sunlight caught in stray wisps
of hair, and even a touch of indulgence
in the half smile and arched eyebrow
that seemed to ask, "What are you looking at?"

(In Traverse City Mary Mankaja, 19,
plunges up to her elbows in the soapy water
back in the kitchen of the Lake Cafe.
She's only been doing this a week and figures
maybe two more to save enough for a ticket
back to the Canyon. When she gets to Peach Springs,
she'll telephone and somebody will bring horses
up to Hualapai Hilltop to get her. She sees
the whole trip down, back and forth on the
switchbacks until they get to the Canyon floor.
Then the twin columns of Wigleeva Rocks,
and there will be the Creek and she'll
be home. She throws a pot into the rinse sink.
This didn't turn out, but she'll get back.
Tourists have been coming to Havasupai
since she was as big as a gopher, and why
this time did she get involved? Because Fernando
had studied—what was it, you know, tribes
and their cultures. He was Chicano, born

in Las Cruces. Had gone to college, but was
different from Anglos, not stupid. So when
he asked her to come with him, she thought about it.
She'd been outside to school but never far away.
He said she ought to see things at least. There's not
that much to do in the Canyon, except cooking
and laundry and swimming at the Falls, and an old
movie once a week at the Recreation Center
about whites against Indians. Nobody in Supai
has any money to travel. So she said yes.
Didn't come home from the trip up to the Rim,
just telephoned and told them she was leaving.
Mother said, "We'll be here." It was fun at first.
They went to Phoenix and ate in restaurants.
In the motel room he would tell her to stand
in the middle of the bed and hold her hair up
over her head and he would just look. It felt
as though she had flown up into the stars
next to the moon and could stay if she wanted to.
But meanwhile there was the table next to the bed,
with a lamp and an ashtray and a bottle of lotion.
Through the window she could see his white Dart
in the parking lot. So she was still on earth.
He took her to dance bars, but she was too shy.
A lot of it scared her. When waitresses would ask,
"Where are y'all from?" she didn't want to say.
One night he got drunk and told her he had a wife.
He hadn't seen her for a long time and didn't think
they could get back together. He admitted being
confused and said it was from trying to live
in two different worlds. He didn't know what
he was going to do when his money ran out.
It went down from there. He wasn't the only thing
she didn't understand. It was embarrassing.
She had to explain that growing up in the Canyon

in a way had been very protective, a lot
on the outside seemed stupid and you missed
having your people around you, even though sometimes
they were boring. She misses them now and wishes
she were walking down the main street, her feet
in the warm dust, the cottonwoods giving shade,
the green smell of their leaves in the air,
the shadow of a horse moving across the ground. . . .
Anyway, one night they drove into Traverse City
and found a motel, and he got real serious. He said
it was time for them to split up, he had to go
back home. She cried. He spoke soft to her and held her,
but her heart had turned into a rock. She got up,
told him to give her twenty dollars, which he did,
and she walked out, just like that. When she has
that feeling of being on the right track, she never
worries, she knows it will come out in a good way.
Maybe it was good she got a chance to see it all.
She'll be back in time for Peach Festival,
the kids will be going away to school, she'll tell
them a couple of things to watch out for, and life
will turn back to the way it's always been.
She doesn't care if she never gets married, either,
as long as the water of the Havasu is green and cool.)

16.

1989

I'm driving back to New York from Cambridge
with S. and J. after our weekend retreat
with the brothers of Saint John the Evangelist.
No snow, but gray midwinter skies match the overall
cold and damp. After an hour of lighthearted
or searching comments, we've turned attention
inward to sort things out. Passing through
Providence—factory chimneys, white steeples—
the name alone makes me review what probably
is an insoluble doctrine. Freedom of will
doesn't mean we aren't at every crossroads
being looked out for. Think of these highways,
the passing lanes, white-on-green signage,
constant decision-making on the part of all
who travel them, some few united in the joint
project of safety. Through accident and choice,
we make a life that proves to be intended.
Good, but what is being worked out now as I
return to difficulties waiting at home?
Not at home: I'm staying at a friend's
apartment till I find somewhere to live.
(Advice to those about to separate:
Have a room of your own before announcing
departure.) Typical of the band who follow
where feeling leads, I'd laid no plans, and so
am now caught up in a stiff, corrective phase,
studying charts and skies in the storm's wake.

A flock of birds wheels over the distant field
and magically settles each on a bare branch
of a widespread tree. And the very hairs of my head
are numbered. . . . When the towers of the city
slip into view, windows lighting up their golden

geometries, I think of all who have lived
and died there, of all the lights on Broadway. . . .
Never a place for the dull or faint of heart,
let it give me the grit to see this through.

(Larayne Beason, formerly of Lenox Avenue,
makes her way down Ninth, below 42nd Street,
leaning forward, pushing a shopping cart ahead.
Spanish man gave it to her, said he didn't need it.
She wasn't ready to chunk her clothes and stuff,
and it holds the soda cans she's picked up to sell.
Doesn't know how long she can keep the thing.
They won't let you bring it in Port Authority,
and the other day when she was going up
to the Welfare office, she had to take a bus,
so she asked a sister seemed like she didn't go
nowhere if she'd watch it for her, and she did—
but might not the next time. The Welfare lady
said don't give up, keep coming back, it will work
out soon, but she's not so sure, one week on the street
has like to run her crazy already. You never know
when people come up to you what they going to do.
One old fool jumped her where she was sleeping
on her pallet over the subway grating next
to the Chemical Bank. She slipped out from under
and screamed, If he didn't get away she was
going to lay a brickbat upside his head, old fool.
Must have scared him, because he hightailed it.
She didn't sleep a wink the rest of the night,
and that's it, you can't get no sleep on the street.
How you supposed to take care of your business?
You forget where you are. Like, see, she found
this pack of cigarettes. Got on the bus and without
thinking just lit one up. She was sitting next
to this white lady said, "Miss, you're not supposed

to smoke here," and she just automatically snapped,
"It's a lot of things you're not supposed to do you do,"
and then the lady jerked her coat up like, This trash
is going to spill ashes on me, so then she got mad
and yelled, "Don't worry lady, I ain't going to burn
your purple coat." Course the bitch complained
to the driver and they put her off. This would not
have happened in the old days. But you just lose it,
you know? Lot of these people out here are gone, child,
ain't nobody upstairs, no use knocking on the door.
That's what scares her. That she'll just drift away,
she won't know where or who she is and won't give a
damn. The cart bumps over the curb as they cross
39th. She wants to get down to that church
where homeless get a free dinner. If she spends
the night down there, she can get early on the line.
Don't know that neighborhood, where to go,
where to sleep, but she'll figure it out.
Lord God, what is going to be the end of this?
While she's waiting for the light, a man
with a black hat and long beard comes up
and says, "Here's something," without her even
asking. She says, "Bless you," and pushes on.)

17.

1990

My month in the Santa Cruz Mountains at an end
I'd begun the solo homeward trip with a steady
twelve-hour pull the first day. In Sacramento
protesters on the steps of the Capitol waved signs
demanding wider literacy (and let me add
another voice to those that cried *Venceremos!*).

I-80 climbs high into the Nevada Range,
up where timber thins out near Donner Pass,
the skies cloudless and pure as spring water.
I exited at Truckee for a short detour
down to Lake Tahoe, not quite destroyed yet
by condos, malls, and Trader Vics, since almost nothing
can detract from snowcapped mountains mirrored
in receptive blue. (But, oh, for a well-aimed
bulldozer.) The Silver State registers as such
when highway Stop 'n' Shops are stocked with quarter
slot machines, handy for getting rid of loose change.
Who'd be willing, though, to miss the real thing,
and not get off at Reno to take a chance on Bally's,
joining anxious swarms of lemmings that pour into
the dim mystique of the hotel lobby? Casino's down
a few steps, a vast catacomb lit with gaudy
neon and rank on marching rank of flashing lights. . . .
They are there still, grandmothers and Second War vets
playing blackjack or pumping slots, the jingle
of coin punctuating proceedings as three kings
or cherries line up for paydirt. "Um, five tokens, please."
But when the fourth one hit, I cashed them in and fled,
as though canceling a courtship with disaster.

Nevada desert was a different prospect, traffic
at sunset minimal, a limitless terrain bare

of vegetation so that subtle mineral colors
crept out and constantly revised themselves
under the shifting play of angled light.
So far no one's seen fit to build at the foot
of the Humboldt Range, sierra remaining just
as it was in the beginning, a reservoir
of unparaphrasable content not qualified
by human intrusion, deepening as the tide
of night advanced and early stars pricked
the blue-to-green canvas stretched overhead.

After a few days, travel's dawn-to-dusk
arc of highway's no interruption to dreams
from the previous night, one speechless
ambient, always forward, fragments of a life
composing specimen years projected over
receding playbacks in the outside rearview
(its caption warning daytime sleepers that
OBJECTS IN MIRROR APPEAR CLOSER THAN THEY ARE),
until at last the pattern clarifies—though not
made manifest apart from varied contexts
assembled in collage, since character
has power to discover, over time,
expressive form within blank incident,
just as the lodestone can enchant a dust
of iron filings into the figure of a rose.

In this case, the compass rose, nor were travels
yet at their end. A scraping tumbleweed
caught under the car snapped me to attention
in North Platte, NE, where after a pit stop
common sense said no more driving today, and here
was The Lonesome Pine Motel.
                              Long nights in transit,

sparked up only by brief, stammering calls
to you, keeping watch in Ohio. After which,
an inventory never sufficiently varied:
brass lamp suspended from its chain, frying
TV, the brown shag rug and Ivory soap-leaves,
an old codger coughing up ice somewhere outside,
muffled cries and flushings consubstantial
with the darkness. . . . It has all blended
into one persistent habitation, The Room,
entered and vainly checked out of over
and again, impassive cradle for how many
tossings and turnings, how many standoffs
with the mirror, how many local news briefs
on Lions Club fundraisers for the deaf. . . .

State after state from the past brought into
the foreground. Ann and I once again sort out
colors of the thermal springs of Yellowstone,
drive up just in time to see Old Faithful
transform internal pressures into a huge plume
of energetic steam. Or Walter will pitch the tent
in Promised Land Valley, up in the Poconos.
And I will cross the Mississippi, leaving behind
the white columns and wrought iron of Vicksburg.
Sometimes the radio's what turns back the clock—
now, for instance, when a newscaster announces
this morning that Sarah Vaughan has died, up floats
the woman guide at Whitman's house in Camden,
who looked like her. (Part of a trip two years
ago to Key West, the morning after a night
spent with Sandy's parents in Haverford.)
Directly opposite the county jail, the house
sat in a rundown sector of a depressed city.
Gesturing, combing a hand through her hair,

she mused with chiding fondness about someone
who might have been a slightly dotty uncle,
nevertheless, a genius. We could see the pain
of bereavement hadn't yet healed. Whispering,
she pointed out his tan Quaker hat preserved
in a glass case. Our greatest poet. . . . And now,
the FM station begins its half-hour tribute
by playing Vaughan's "Lullaby of Birdland."

Here's Minneapolis. Fair Cantonese
cooking served at a tourist-oriented
restaurant on Washington Avenue.
Order taken, why not fill the time by inventing
a life for the waiter?—the other one, I mean,
head propped, my fingers drumming on the tablecloth.
He comes from Kodiak Island, Alaska. Is
Eskimo. Grew up in the shadow of the old
Russian Orthodox church steeple there
and was taught by the priest. What's more,
entered seminary himself but decided
he didn't have a calling. Part of him
wants to go back home, but his girlfriend
has urged him to stay. She likes her job
at the Parks Department and only hopes he can
find work more rewarding than waiting tables.

When he brings the stainless covers, our eyes
meet and I'm tempted to ask for the actual
story. But of course say nothing. Instead,
revisit his island and hear a bell clanking
out Sunday morning across the frozen harbor
as late November mists hover over rooftops. . . .
Since invention also has an ache, an aura,
possibly something could be done with this?

After the meal, a drive down to the suspension
bridge, spotlit, thick with traffic whizzing over
from St. Paul. In midwinter, two decades back,
many finely tuned torments came to an end here.
Loss of rhyme, loss of life. Always a long shot
the bare, forked artist must be willing to risk
in the face of natural and human indifference,
the minus nine degrees receptiveness of both.
Always, too, a fought-for claim the wording of it
makes one's mind something more than one more case,
a safe-conduct into the world of light.

(Elizabeth Krieger of Wausau has come with her little
girl Marcia to sit at the bedside of her dying aunt
in St. Paul. As a present she brought a small piece
of needlework made by the Hmong people, who came
as refugees to Wisconsin from Southeast Asia.
It's a sort of appliqué, where various beasts
drink at a spring in the Peaceable Kingdom.
Aunt Ramona was born in Ephraim, up on Green Bay,
and they're all Moravian stock originally.
She's quite prepared to go, but glad that Betty came
to say goodbye. She listens to the news, all about
troubles with the Chippewa, who want to maintain
their spearfishing rights up at Lac du Flambeau
but have been called names and attacked by local
resisters. They think it's not fair and will ruin
line fishing—which it may well do, but the law
is the law. Marcia is fidgeting, so Aunt Ramona
tells Betty to give her a chocolate from the box
on the nighttable. Marcia chews a caramel and looks
at the yellow box, printed with letters she can't
read yet. But there are colored pictures—
a bluebird, flowers, a little pink house—but shaped
funny, out of little squares, like when water stays

on a windowscreen. Down in one corner is a brown dog
with straight legs. Pretty flowers, but she likes
the bird better. On the back, other flowers, birds,
and a ship, with pointed flags. Mama isn't looking.
She takes another candy, which melts in her mouth
like jelly. They keep talking. Her foot itches.
She whispers a song as she takes the shoe off,
scratches, then has trouble getting it back on.
"What are you doing, Marcia?" Mama puts the shoe on
and takes her into her lap. She was a late child,
the others are all off at college now, except John.
No hesitation, though, about having her when the test
came back. Tom was all for it. Still, in a way she felt
she'd outgrown the whole thing, even though every step
was so familiar. She felt a cramp or two and then
the water broke right while she was cooking supper.
Tom telephoned ahead, people were expecting them,
and it so happened Dr. Grossman was at the hospital.
She just felt a bit ridiculous going through it again,
feet in the stirrups, and having pain that, gracious,
you can't keep quiet about, however you try, like having
your breath squeezed out through a wringer. A big mess,
but that's part of it, and the nurses are so helpful.
The doctor put in the stitches, which anesthesia
didn't quite handle, but she got through it. And then
Marcia as red as an apple, but real quiet, quieter
than her brothers had been. There *is* something rare
about having a little girl, she's very glad she did.
It was like setting the clock back to the time
when Tom and she were just starting out, his first
years in the furniture business. He'd been secretary
for the Republican Club, made a lot of friends, then
resigned after Watergate because he said Nixon had
betrayed the principles of the party. Later on, Ford
reconciled him to it. Those were such days. Easier now.

Marcia was with her when she'd driven up to the Hmong
to see what they had. The lady who sold the needlework
also had a little girl and it made such a bond
between them, even with the fact that her English
was skimpy and all. They have beautiful deep dark eyes,
and do such intricate work. Oh. Marcia's climbed up
next to Aunt Ramona and given her a hug. It pushes
her glasses off center, "Marcia, be careful!" but
a smile breaks across the soft, wrinkled face,
maybe it's all right—oh, but wait, Marcia has
chocolate smeared all over her hands. "Marcia!
Let Mother wipe your hands!" and Aunt Ramona laughs.
Then straightens her glasses, smoothes her hair, coughs,
and says, "It's time for Garrison Keillor's program.")

18.

1991

Doubletakes from every listener when I mention
plans to watch the tickertape parade New York
is throwing for veterans of Operation
Desert Storm. You have to work and wouldn't
in any case have bothered, but R., in town
for a few days, has agreed to come along,
to see how the Zeitgeist is blowing these days.
Not since the era when JFK told us
to "ask what we could do for our country"
(how many betrayals and exposés ago)
has naive sponsorship of U.S. government
and all its works been possible; in fact,
a balance sheet of our history tips sadly
toward the negative—in the judgment of many
thoughtful products of that history, who need
not fear reprisals for what they say or print,
or indeed any lasting attention paid at all.
Granted mistakes, and that the past is past,
what now? Seems nearly everyone has settled
into resignation—well, except these here,
cheering and waving flags and proud to be
boosters of the winning team. Here it comes,
a blizzard of paper tribute, flung by bushels
from highrise windows, the air rights of this
hot June morning transformed into a colloidal
suspension of bright-colored bits, shot through
with sinuous paper serpents, all trembling,
alive, a speechless tidal wave given voice
by roars from multitudes driven to frenzy
by the smiling passage of top brass, marching bands,
squadrons of youth in speckled camouflage,
every sign of military might that could be mustered,
short of restaged battles on native ground.

Each dazzled, wondering face, each uplifted arm,
belongs to lives whose names I'll never know,
a whole populace jammed just this once together,
wearing the camouflage of unity. What in it
recalls that day we boarded a prop plane for D.C.
(ten years now) to attend a function the Carters
gave at the White House for American poetry?
Only that here are two versions of the need to
find meaning in the fact of nationality.
Representative poets read their works to us
in several rooms, milled around, avoiding some,
greeting others, taking stances. Later I had a moment
to banter with the Chief about our native state. . . .
Perhaps if all of these here had the chance to "read"
their lives aloud, our import for each other—
whether to slip away, nod, or embrace—just might
come clear. Confetti, cheers, Souza. Beer cans
held aloft. Police barriers. Anonymity.
One more impracticable American Dream.

(Cathy Pisano hangs on to Bashir's arm
as they move through the crowd. She wishes
they hadn't come to the parade, but he said
he really wanted to see. They'd visited
the new Mosque this morning, which she'd liked
fairly well—anyway, it was important for her
to learn about these things because she and Bashir
will probably marry once he finishes his thesis
at Columbia on Islamic practice in Pakistan.

She'd tried, briefly, to explain about Slick:
How they'd been best friends at Borromeo High
in Newark, two snotty teenagers in their pleated
skirts, white socks and saddle oxfords. They weren't
that much alike, really. Slick was a tomboy, bravest

girl in the school, sometimes reckless. There was
a Sister they called Consummation because the word
was always popping out of her mouth in the weirdest
contexts, either as a noun or verb. She taught
American History, and it just got funnier the more
she'd say things like "The first explorers
consummated a European wish to acquire new lands
and resources," or "The Union of the Thirteen
Colonies reached consummation only with the signing
of the Constitution." The day came she said it once
too often, and Slick busted out laughing, which
dragged Cathy with her. They got into even
more trouble by refusing to explain what was so
hilarious. Had to stay after school for a week,
Acts of Contrition, awful. Which made them closer.
Times she'd go over to Slick's house, her father
reading the paper, with a Mario Lanza record playing
in the background, her mother rattling on about
the upcoming novena. And there was a little
blue vase sitting on top of the television
with Italian and American flags stuck in it.
When her parents bought Slick a used Camaro,
they drove down to Atlantic City and then
to New York, to wait in line at the clubs.
After Cathy moved to New York and got work
with Amnesty, they sort of lost touch, though
she knew Slick went out for a while with a guy
who was a roadie for Guns N' Roses. Then a letter
came saying she was enlisting. That was the last.
They'd been drifting further and further apart,
really. But, when the news program last March
mentioned some of the casualties were women,
and gave her name, Cathy was horrified. Killed.
They never got a chance to say goodbye. She gazes
absentmindedly all around her, so many people,

why are they here, could they possibly know?
This is crazy, pieces of colored paper in shapes—
a red heart, a black bat, a star, a crescent moon—
and suddenly she's crying, out of control, she
grabs Bashir, and buries her head on his shoulder,
God help us, darling Slick, cheated of her life.)

19.

1989

I'd started out in Saratoga Springs
and taken I-90 west, through the Finger Lakes,
Seneca Falls, all the way to Buffalo.
On Enola Ave., in the ghetto, a shirtless boy,
eight or nine, held up a placard that said,
"Car wash $.30," and an Exxon attendant
gave me directions for Art Park (that encounter
of American sculpture with open American air).
The viewing platform over the plunging river
put the idea in my head to revisit the Falls,
which Ann and I had seen from Canada just twenty
years ago. So, after finding a motel on Grand Island
and having my dinner, I drove up to see it.
All changed. Spotlights kept the torrent visible
while amplifiers from the mall galvanized
the night with Handel's "Water Music," a neon
light-show synesthetically echoing each
counterpointed voice. Now for a broad, slow rainbow
projected across the cataract so good taste
might be once again defeated utterly.
Crowds upon crowds of viewers laughing,
talking—Latino, Japanese-, English-, Polish-
American—thrilled to be there with the children
for this popular epiphany freely espoused
in the land of liberty. How free was I?
Free enough to forgo a reflex groan and to
allow that human happiness is various,
that no one has everything—nor could I in all
solemnity have taken them along earlier
in the day to gaze at a ziggurat of rusted
oildrums titled "Drums Along the Niagara,"
to mention only one work in the exhibition.

Morning. Mild sunlight along Lake Erie,
a Mediterranean shore with vineyards
and red-tiled roofs that bespeak Italy
as much as the Great Lakes. I'm on my way
to Indiana, hope to make Columbus, OH,
by nightfall. Overlapping geographies
unpack their stories: one about returning
East more than a year ago on I-70,
a pause to have a look at Martin's Ferry,
where Roebling's first suspension bridge connects
the town to Wheeling, WV. Plainspoken names,
unmemorialized outside the aggrieved
dreamwork of James Wright—who also found
a latter-day beatitude among the vineyards
and pines of Tuscany before he came back home
to die.
        Telescoped time-frames: could I foresee,
as I circled Ohio's capital city that night,
I'd be living there the following year,
you coming up from Cincinnati every weekend
to survey the world together from our top floor
on Jefferson Avenue? Or set off again on joint
excursions—to Chicago, for the Lyric Opera,
or Columbus (the Indiana one), where classic
modern buildings commissioned the past
five decades form an ideal urban habitat.
From now forward these interstates will read
as a palimpsest, a layered narrative
for the portable home entertainment center
consciousness is, the fluent, interior
Niagara. . . .
        It rains, the sun rises and sets
on the just and the unjust. Two days more, and here
was New Harmony, down in the southwest corner
of Indiana, on the banks of the Wabash, a grid

of streets lined with golden raintrees brought
from Mexico during the last century. Half
a month in a restored house, with no duties
except daily self-assigned hours at the desk.
Notes for "La Madeleine." A translation project.

But not all day. One afternoon I drove to see
Angel Mound State Park, site of an ancient town
built by the Middle Mississippian Culture
and abandoned during the fourteen hundreds.
Furnace heat, shrilling cicadas, sluggish river.
A line of oaks in the distance, high Temple Mound
with reconstructed sanctuary, windowless.
Inside, glints of light slipped through the thatching.
A baked clay basin for fires. Presence of the dead.
The sense of being watched, my thinking overheard,
sifted, to know which blessing ought to be conferred.

And back in town, having made some headway, there
was time to have a meal at the house of the last
descendant bearing the surname of Robert Owen—
who wore his eighty-six years serenely, pleased
to talk about Kentucky horses, the Saratoga
track, and the way things went before the war.

(Al Carson, 46, of Indianapolis
has come down with his wife to spend a few days
with her sister. He can take off any old time now,
since he's been on disability for a year.
Before, he worked in a die-cast factory
for automobile parts. The robots in the electric-
hydraulic system broke, spilled some oil
that caught fire. He and the others got out,
but not before they breathed enough smoke
to choke a horse. When the foreman told him,

Report for work tomorrow, the plant would be
operating again, they almost went knuckle junction,
except he was too weak. Not well yet, and will he
ever be? His wife Barbara got part-time work
at a day-care center, to help make ends meet.
At least the kids are grown. Bobby Jo works
at the Southroads Mall out in Tulsa,
and Al Jr. has gone to help his granddad,
who runs a service station in Willow Springs,
Missouri. He's a boy likes country ways,
and it's true there's no more beautiful land
than the Ozarks. Al wishes he could go back,
but Barbara has family, friends and church
in Indianapolis, she's president of her
Eastern Star chapter, and says, Let's please stay,
she never specially cared for the Show Me State.
No, and Al's not too crazy about her sister Myra,
either, but this old house of hers has lots of room,
and it makes a change to come down. Nothing much
to do, of course. He went with them yesterday
to buy groceries, said he'd get some bananas.
But it's hard to find any that aren't either
green or rotten nowadays. As he was picking
through them, Myra came up and said, "Come on, Al,
you're not buying a Cadillac," which she thought
was real cute. He got even later on, though.
When she washed her hair and put it in curlers,
he pointed and asked, "What channels do you get?"
"More than you do," is all she said. Man don't work,
women don't respect him, simple as that. He just
can't get his strength back. Doesn't even want
to go to the 500 any more. Doctor says,
Be patient, and that's what he is, a patient. Damn
hot today. He goes to the screen door and looks out
in the back yard, where Barbara aims the garden

hose on her nephew Harold, stampeding around
in a green swimsuit and yelling like an Apache.
On impulse, Al steps out on the porch and down
to the lawn, takes the hose from Barbara, who says
"What on earth," as he douses his head with water. . . .
She smiles, wipes his forehead, just like the good old days.
Hands the boy the hose and laughs, "Let's go inside, Al.")

20

1992

Dolores and Wayne Davis have retired and are living in a condo in St. Croix. Their son Herbert manages the citrus groves from an office in Tampa. This October afternoon, their grandson knocks on a door in Ybor City, pays, gets his bag, returns to the car, drives to his girlfriend's apartment. She says she bleached the works while he was gone, so they are ready to use. His father picks up the phone and dials

Mike Kovich has been managing a hardware store in The Dalles for ten years. He has remarried and has one son. His daughter Amber visited in August and has gone back to her husband in Wichita. Connie married a highway contractor years ago and is doing volunteer work for elementary school literacy in Salt Lake. Mike wonders whether

Cal and Theresa Svenborg live in Twin Falls. Their son John-boy was born with Down's syndrome and needs a lot of attention. Cal's mother is now in a nursing home in Twin Falls because her Parkinson's disease has gotten worse. He's feeling a lot of pressure from dealing with all this. Theresa compares it to the time

After Yvonne moved back in, she and Rosetta Haines lived together in Atlanta for many years, until Rosetta died of a heart attack. Yvonne's son George, who went to Ohio State on a football scholarship, is on the coaching staff at Georgia Tech, is married and has two sons. One of them

Ray LaNoue's father died last spring. He is on the Louisiana circuit this week and drove into New Orleans earlier today. He always stays with the Franciscans over on North Miro Street, since hotels are so expensive in the city. The Father has invited him to an evening service, part of a week-long devotion preparing for the Feast of St. Luke. Dinner comes after. He puts through a telephone call to Diane, who is visiting a cousin of hers who lives in Kitty Hawk, North Carolina. The kids are staying with

Isabel Ramos has just returned from a week in San Juan, Puerto Rico, where she had a wonderful time sightseeing with Hiram Gonzales, whom she's been with six months now. Her brother José meets her at Newark Airport to tell her their mother has died in a car accident. The family moved to Paterson back in the '70s. They drive directly to the Funeraria Las Americas on Madison, Isabel sobbing and saying that she and José are now orphans. Hiram takes her hand and

Mathilda Vallabriga's father died. She has moved to Lisbon to be nearer her daughter's family, but keeps the house in Old Lyme for occasional visits home. Actually, she plans

Billy Barstow has his own architectural firm in Baltimore. He lives with an English professor at Johns Hopkins. Henry Barstow had them visit at the farm in the Valley, but hasn't been willing to come to them in Baltimore. He has had to sell off a few acres of bottom land to keep the place. Lately, he's been experimenting with a new

Walker Tuggs had his first retrospective at the Carnegie-Mellon Gallery in Pittsburgh, a catalogue and monograph printed to go with it. He has no plans to move from Columbiana, but he is painting again. The thing about landscape is

Martha Diodati died six years ago, and her house on Chestnut Street has been bought by a California couple who own a food-importing concern, involving trips back and forth between

Gene Gerard lives in Lewiston, and has been in AA nearly seven years now. His wife Marilynne works for New England Telephone, and he's still at Ace Roofing, "One day at a time," he says. On weekends he helps out with the Lewiston Little League. It occurred to him

Chuck Yuen runs an audio store in the Haight, lives over it with his Vietnamese lover. They just got back from a trip to mainland China, where they both came down with bronchitis, but had a great time even so, and now that they're home, they've recovered. His father had begun

Victor Lopez is on a business trip to Morelia in Mexico. His wife Sharon is doing well, with a job in development at the Kimbell Museum. Becky has one more year at school and Sam is in his first term at Kenyon. It's a brilliant day, with blue skies and a few racing clouds moving east. Sharon notices

Kevin Shanahan died of lung congestion brought on by Kaposi's sarcoma last summer. Kimberley Sternberg has moved to a smaller apartment in Los Feliz. She's biding her time while Todd's divorce gets worked out. Meanwhile he pulled strings and got her work as assistant to a casting director at Paramount, which she likes a lot. She misses Kevin, and is planning to go to Honolulu with one of his friends as soon as she

Mary Mankaja was thrown from a horse last month and broke her leg. She's mending and her son is helping with the chores. She almost never leaves Supai any more. But her husband Peter does, since he's been appointed to deal with the State Government. It wasn't the horse's fault, its hoof slipped on a rock in the creek and she was thrown. Next year

Elizabeth Krieger has returned to Wausau after her aunt's death. Her son John was named valedictorian of the senior class. Marcia is in kindergarten and they think she may have dyslexia. Some of the Hmong people were invited to the church last week to tell their stories and share a dinner. They were shy and didn't say much, but everyone seemed to enjoy the occasion. She's been reading a book about

Cathy Pisano and Bashir Ahmed, after a series of disagreements, decided not to see each other for a while—but haven't ruled out the possibility of getting back together later on. He has defended his dissertation and is teaching first-year Arabic at Columbia. Cathy went home to Newark and ran into Slick's parents at the mall, who looked a lot older. They said they would always be proud of their daughter. Why is it

Al Carson's health has improved and he is doing house-painting in Indianapolis. His wife was kept on at the day-care center and has returned from a visit with her daughter in Tulsa. Her nephew Harold worked as a lifeguard this summer at the pool in Harmonie State Park. He's good at basketball and

Almost forgotten by everyone who ever knew her, Larayne Beason is sitting on a park bench facing Hudson Street, next to her bag of clothes. She's not sure where she is. A large cut on her forehead is clotted with dried blood, but she doesn't notice it. She wears running shoes with no socks. Sores on her legs. She looks at a leaf on the ground and thinks, Winter be here soon. Scared. Who is that lying on the bench? She is talking in a low voice to herself, pleading, because she is the only one who will listen, but

You came to New York in January of last year, and you plan to stay, for better or for worse, richer, poorer, in sickness and in health. The day begins with you, ends with you. This first year of bereavement in the aftermath of my father's death. Late summer sees us take a long walk down from Columbus Circle all the way to Washington Square, and, look, the fountain sends up a high, foaming pillar of water. . . . Your thirty-fifth birthday falls in mid-October, and what we're going to do